A PEACE OF MIND IS BETTER THAN A PIECE OF MAN

(2025 NEW EDITION)

RUTH HAMPTON

RUTH HAMPTON WRITES, LLC

AUTHOR'S NOTE

This fictional novel is dedicated to victims and their loved ones associated with domestic violence or those who may be or have been in a toxic relationship. If you feel you are in an abusive or toxic relationship, then please seek professional help immediately.

This is a work of fiction. Names, characters, places, and incidents either are the product of the author's imagination or are used fictitiously. Any resemblance to actual persons, living or dead, events or locales, is entirely coincidental.

Disclaimer: Ruth Hampton, the author, is not of the medical profession and does not claim to be; therefore, you are not obligated to take her advice...be persuaded by your own mind.

CONTENTS

PREFACE

Toxic Relationships

Toxic relationships can be extremely damaging to one's mental and emotional health and overall well-being. These types of relationships can often start out great but quickly spiral into something toxic and dangerous. Signs of these types of relationships include constant fighting, gaslighting, and manipulation. It's important to recognize these signs and take action to remove oneself from the relationship before it becomes too detrimental. Seek help from a trusted support network if you find yourself in a toxic relationship.

One of the biggest challenges can be recognizing when a relationship has become toxic and knowing how to address it. It's important to establish healthy communication habits early on in a relationship to prevent toxic behavior from taking root.

Clarification of:

Fighting?: Fighting in a toxic relationship is never easy. It can be physical violence (hitting or pushing) and/or verbal abuse. It can feel like a constant battle where both partners are trying to gain the upper hand.

This type of relationship can take a toll on a person's mental health and self-esteem. Despite this, it can also be difficult to break away from the relationship, as the toxic partner may have a hold on the other person. Fighting in a toxic relationship is an incredibly difficult and emotionally draining experience. It can leave one feeling trapped, hopeless, and lost. The constant bickering, arguing, and hurtful words can take a toll on one's mental health and lead to depression and anxiety. Verbal abuse in a toxic relationship looks like a lot of different things. It can be as subtle as snarky comments and backhanded compliments or as overt as screaming and name-calling. Regardless of the form it takes, verbal abuse is never acceptable in a healthy relationship. Often concealed behind a façade of love and care, the abuser uses verbal abuse as a means of control and domination over their partner. It can cause serious emotional harm, destroy self-esteem, and even lead to physical abuse. Despite this, many individuals stay in toxic relationships due to fear, guilt, or a mistaken belief that they can change their partner.

Gaslighting?: This is when one person tries to convince the other that their perceptions of reality are incorrect, often leading the victim to doubt their own sanity. It can be difficult to recognize gaslighting when you're in the midst of it, but it's important to be aware of this tactic and seek professional help if you suspect it's happening to you. Remember, you are not crazy or imagining things - gaslighting is a real and harmful form of abuse.

Manipulation?: One form of manipulation is using guilt to control the victim, often by making them feel responsible for the abuser's behavior. Additionally, abusers may isolate their partners from friends and family, making it harder for them to seek support or leave the relationship.

If you feel you are in an abusive relationship, please seek help immediately.

Disclaimer: Ruth Hampton, the author, is not of the medical profession and does not claim to be; therefore, you are not obligated to take her advice...be persuaded by your own mind.

ACKNOWLEDGEMENT

~Firstly, I want to thank God the Father, God the Son, and the Holy Spirit for giving me the gift of being a writer and on becoming a self-published author.

~Secondly, I want to thank my children (Joshua and Jasmyne) and my grandkids (Alayziah, Ma'Kiyah, Lorenzo, and Lamarco) for being my strongest supporters and reasons behind my authorship. Praying to leave this legacy for them.

~Thirdly, I thank my parents Elijah Hampton, Sr.(d eceased) and Mae Covington-Hampton for birthing me and giving me their personality traits: Dad (humor, ambition, open mindedness, happy-go-lucky attitude, friendliness; leadership); Mom (strong faith, humor, leadership, patience, ambition, friendliness).

~Fourthly, I thank my siblings, nieces, and nephews for sticking with me and always having my back!

~Finally, I thank my special friends who stick by me listening to my cries, complaints, defeats, and successes without judgment.

PROLOGUE

"Seriously? You think you leaving me?!" Elliot yells.

His eyes are full of anger...piercing my very soul. His face is tight. He begins pacing in a circle.

"Did you forget 'til death do us part'? You know I'm not letting you go, right? I'm ready to go join my family, Rayna, and you going with me. You're part of my family. It's time for you to meet my mom, dad, and Elijah."

He walked slowly toward me. Face tight. Fist balled up. He quickly ran to the bedroom and returned with a black, leather belt.

Frantically, I tried to explain that I couldn't take living with him anymore and that everyone was talking about him killing some of his relatives.

But it was as though he could no longer hear or see me; as if he was in some hypnotic state. His eyes looked glazed over with evil.

"Elliot!" He was still walking slowly toward me; zombielike. "Elliot! Did you hear what I said?"

Fist closed. He raises the belt. It was wrapped tightly around his fist like brass knuckles. My body was trembling now. I was frozen stiff. My legs wouldn't budge. I couldn't scream! "Run!" I heard my mind telling me, but fear gripped me. I couldn't move. I felt as though I was weighed down by

heavy sandbags. I haven't seen him this angry before. And
then...

INTERPRETATION

*D*isclaimer: This is the author's interpretation or opinion of what is believed to be "a piece of or half a man." The author's interpretation or opinion is not meant to shame, slander, or slay a man's character but hopefully the examples within the books will point out ways an abuser or one who may not realize he's abusive (without being physical) can/will change his behavior as pleasing to God.

Author's Opinion: "a piece of a man" or "half a man: an unstable and/or insecure male who does not and/or may refuse to follow the leadership of God. He simply brings no spiritual value or harmonious equality to the relationship, instead he instills fear to dominate and/or control his spouse or significant other.

WORD of GOD for the believers of HIS WORD: I Peter 3:7; 1Corinthians 6:9-11 and 7:2-5; Hebrews 13:4; Genesis 2:18-24; Ephesians 5:22-33

When you read the scriptures concerning marriage, God styled the marriage as the church. God is supposed to be the head of human life. HE meant for the man to be head of the household and left scripture and guidelines for him to lead his family spiritually, emotionally, and honorably.

You will not find in God's Word that a woman should be: (a) re-raised as a child by her husband or significant other;

(b) used as a punching bag or door mat; and/or (c) spoken to as a regurgitated-filled garbage can.

CHAPTER 1

RAYNA JENNINGS

"Ray-Ray, get up from outta dat bed! It's time to go to church! Dis da Lord's day and I don't wanna be late. C'mon here and pick me up!"

"Okay, Grandma. I'm almost finished. You know this diva got to look her best on the Lawd's day!"

"*Almost finished*? Chile, I hope no man ain't causing you to be late for Jesus! You know God's got His eye on you!" If you don't hurry up I'm gone stand out by da mailbox and hitch a ride."

"C'mon Grandma! I'll be there. Besides my '*man*' and his ol' clunker already left. He had to hurry home to help his Mom with something." Ray-Ray said while rolling her eyes.

"I show hope you prayed about him, and ain't shackin' up'! He need to go to church with ya."

"Yes, ma'am Grandma. Love you, love you, love you!"

I always do that to her when I'm not trying to listen. It's my way of not arguing or talking back to her.

I'm so grateful that Grandpa Harry was sweet enough to leave me an inheritance once I graduated from college as a registered nurse. I was able to purchase this townhouse and a car.

Ain't that something? The field of nursing; just like Grandma. What are the odds that we both work at Sumnerfield Children's Hospital? I'm a night owl though, and she's the early bird!

In my colossal bedroom window, facing the town park, I opened the blinds and began to reminisce...

CHAPTER 2

GRANDMA FLORENCE AND GRANDPA HAROLD

M y Grandma Flo (a.k.a. Florence Anne Jennings) a 65-year-old pediatric nurse, raised me since I was 10 years old. A very decent living and strict upbringing.

Every Wednesday night Bible study and church service on Sunday mornings at St. John Baptist Church. We lived in a large, luxurious 3-bedroom townhome with a two-car garage. Sumnerfield, North Carolina is a charming, quaint town of about 275,000 residents and 30 miles from Raleigh. Grandma Flo, Mama, and I still live here. But how I miss Grandpa!

Grandpa Harry (a.k.a. Harold Ray Jennings) was a respectable banker of 30 years at Mirren's First Savings Bank and was the first black man to sit on the Board of Directors. He was a proud man and quite the stylish dresser. That's one thing Grandma said she loved about him.

I remember as a little girl, he used to ride me on his back. I was a cowgirl and he was my horse. After church on Sundays, he, Grandma Flo, and I would walk to the park for ice cream at *Frankie's Frozen Treats* ice cream truck. I would play on the playground while they sat and held hands discussing the day's events from church. Flirting publicly on the park bench, Grandma's eyes would flicker and flutter while Grandpa tickled her sides. She would burst out with laughter. Then gently kiss him on his cheek and, he would smile so big. It lit the sky. Sometimes he would tap her butt and she would candidly say, "Now Harold Ray, not in front of the child!"

He died of a massive heart attack at age 56 when I was thirteen. I was numb with grief that day. I have never seen anyone cry so much as Grandma did. She didn't go to work for about a month. Just lay in bed and cry.

Aunt Hilda Mae had to stay with us during that time. Grandma kept holding her heart and screaming, "He gone! My best friend is gone! Harry, I miss you, baby! Lord help me!" I thought *she* was going to have a heart attack.

It was right then and there that I decided that I didn't wanna cry like that over any man. I guess 32 years of being married to someone will cause you to act like that; especially when you loved each other as much as they did.

Mama and Daddy didn't attend the funeral because they were too busy getting high. At least that's what I overheard Grandma and Aunt Hilda Mae talking about at the repass. Regardless, I missed them both terribly.

CHAPTER 3

RAYMOND ANTHONY BROWN & CAROL RYANN JENNINGS

Like many other places in the world, Sumnerfield has certain corners you should steer clear of. Gangs. Drugs. Violence.

Mama and Daddy, both drug addicts, split when I was 5 years old. They never married. They just "*shacked up*" as my Grandma would say.

Grandma says my parents were not always on drugs.

They were high school sweethearts from 10th grade through 12th grade at Sumnerfield High. Mama got pregnant that January before their Senior year of high school at 17 years old. She had me on September 3, 1979, and Grandma and Grandpa helped care for me so that Mama and Daddy could finish high school.

Grandma Flo says Daddy didn't have an easy childhood. Daddy was an only child and was orphaned at age seven. His parents, Helen and Frank, were shot and killed during an armed robbery at Cecil's Convenient Store. He bounced around to various foster homes until age 12 before living with his mom's sister, Aunt Hilda Mae.

My Mama's childhood was filled with love, church, and vacations. She was spoiled rotten...got anything she wanted.

From kindergarten to ninth grade, she went to St. Mary's School for Girls which was one of Sumnerfield's private schools. Grandma said that Mama cried, complained, and pleaded for them to let her go to Sumnerfield High School. They gave in...and then she met my Dad.

Mama and Daddy went to Sumnerfield Community College and took biopharmaceutical classes. Got high-paying jobs at Barnum Pharmaceuticals, Inc. specializing in the manufacturing and production of anxiety and depression medications. Three years later Mama and Daddy were fired for stealing the pills. They spent one year on probation and had to pay fines to the court and the company. Grandma and Grandpa paid for it.

Grandma said Mama and Daddy were using the pills as drugs. She would say, "Shootin' up their arms." That's how their drug habit began. It went from that to heroin.

I still have fond memories of being happy as a child while I was with them though. They always hugged me and told me they loved me. We always sang and danced together in the living room of our tiny two-bedroom apartment. They got me anything I asked for too!

Daddy always played hide-and-seek with me. Taught me how to build model cars. Daddy loved cars; particularly vintage ones. He was pecan tan, handsome, small build, about 6 feet tall, and had dreadlocks on his shoulders. He seemed invincible to me.

Mama used to sit me on her lap and braid my hair while singing. I loved those pretty multicolor bows she would put in my fro. Mama, a beautiful 5 foot 5 medium build, milk chocolate queen, had long dreadlocks past her shoulders. She and I played with dolls and dressed up. She let me put on her heels, jewelry, and makeup. I enjoyed those times with her so much.

I hated it when Mama and Daddy fought over drugs and money. I saw Daddy hit her a couple of times, and later she would say, "A piece of a man is better than no man at all, baby girl. You remember that. You gone need a man to help you with your bills and keep you somewhere to live. Me and your Daddy love you always, and we love each other too. He doesn't mean to hurt me. Everything will work out. You'll see."

I guess it didn't *"work out"* after all. Mama's final straw with Daddy was when he went to get high and left me at the neighbor's apartment who was passed out from boozing all day. That smell almost made me vomit, so I went right back across the hall to our tiny apartment. I was only five years old. Mama was livid when she found me home alone. So, she kicked Daddy out! I cried because I felt I got him in trouble.

After the split, Mama went to rehab for about four months and left. She said she missed me too much. We got along pretty well and she still went to work while dabbling in drugs.

Daddy had been gone for a year and here comes another *'piece of a man.'* Mama explained that she couldn't keep up with bills by herself. I saw this man slap her around a few times too; just like Daddy did. Mama didn't seem to mind. She acted as though it were the norm. **"Slim"** she called him, but I called him *"Slime."* She would always turn to me with that dreadful *'piece of a man's'* speech.

One night, Mama needed a fix so badly that she and *"Slime"* left me home by myself. She told me she was coming

right back and going to bring me a KitKat. Well, she didn't
return, and I never got that KitKat either!

I got my ten-year-old self up the next morning and dressed
for school. I made a mistake and told my best friend, Sierra,
who told the teacher who told the counselor who told the
social worker who called the Department of Social Services.
And that's how I wound up staying with Grandma Flo and
Grandpa Harry.

I really wanted Daddy, but the last time I saw him was
when I was six years old. We met at the park for ice cream.
Daddy kept saying he was so sorry about the way things
turned out. He said he was going away to get well. Too
many bad memories in Sumnerfield. He hugged me and
said he loved me. I think he was in trouble with the law. At
least that's what I overheard Mama telling Grandma Flo at
breakfast one morning.

I thought about Mama and the tears began to roll. I remembered how distraught I was when she didn't come to
my high school or college graduation. I knew she loved me
but she was still feeling guilty about leaving me. I told her
that I loved her and all was forgiven.

I asked Grandma, "What will it take for Mama to see that
I love her no matter what!"

"Baby, we have to pray and let the Lord do His work. We
can't force it. When the time comes, she will talk to you.
Everything will work out. You'll see. Our faith was being
tested. I am praying for your Mama and Daddy that they
will see the errors of their ways and be healed and delivered.
Make sure you still pray for them as well. "Honor thy father
and mother," she reminded me.

CHAPTER 4

TIME FOR CHURCH

O h goodness! Look at the time! My makeup! Focus Rayna! Lord, Grandma is going to be calling again in a minute!

Grandma knows how to make me get up quickly and in a hurry when she mentions "church" or anything about "Jesus!" I know I don't always do what's right, and I am neither perfect. But I know Jesus loves me, and I will serve him with my whole heart (at some point). I'm just not ready right now. I'm only 22 (almost 23), and I don't want to be a hypocrite like Sis. Johnson, the usher, who slept with Deacon Stanfield a few years ago.

At least that's what I overheard Aunt Hilda Mae tell Grandma Flo at my high school graduation dinner.

I hopped into my shiny silver Mustang convertible to pick up Grandma Flo. Since it's a hot day, I unlock the top and tap the button to let it down.

"Grandma, I'm here!" I phoned her from the car. I was decked out and looked good in my cap-sleeved, sheath black dress. Wearing my red pumps. Red and black earrings, necklace, and bangles to match. Black *Givenchy* sunglasses. All were purchased from *Stacy's*.

"All right, coming girl. I just need to put on my heels."

"Grandma, make sure your Dionne Alexander wig ain't on backwards this time please!"

"Girl, please! I already fixed it! Let this top up. I ain't trying to have my wig fly off!"

"That's why I have dreads!" I mumbled under my breath.

"What you say Ray-Ray?"

"Yes ma'am, Grandma. Love you, love you, love you!"

I rolled up the top and started singing along with the radio to Mary Mary's "Shackles".

Surprisingly, Grandma Flo jumped right on in...tapping her feet to the beat. That wig just bobbing.

Chapter 5

Sunday Morning

"Lord, chile, church is packed today for Pastor Johnson's 35th Pastoral Anniversary! I declare why does Hilda Mae have on them purple shoes with that red hat? I'm gone have to talk to her bout her wardrobe."

"She looks fine to me Grandma."

"Where's purple and red in her outfit? She got on a black and white dress. Gold jewelry too! Lord, Hilda Mae!"

"Ain't the anniversary colors red and black? It's okay that she accented them with purple. Don't talk about my auntie like that Grandma. That's your best friend anyway." I said, laughingly.

"That's my point!" said Grandma while struggling to get out of my car.

I feel the hairs on my neck stand up as I sense eyes are watching me from afar. I begin to look around. I don't recognize anyone new. I see most of the regulars. There are a few college students home for the anniversary.

Nobody's new. Weird.

"Hilda Mae! Wait up, chile!" Aunt Hilda Mae waves to me and she and Grandma walk in the church together. Laughing and talking. "I like that outfit, Hilda Mae! You look sharp today girl!"

"Grandma is a trip," I say to myself.

As I get ready to walk in, someone brushes against me nearly knocking me over.

"Excuse me, I'm so sorry beautiful lady."

"Hi, it's okay." I look up at him. Tall, pecan tan, well-dressed, and handsome.

He glances directly into my eyes. Those beautiful light brown-green eyes. Looking right through me. I start to shiver a little. "He's one fine brutha!" I think to myself.

"Um, I guess I better get on in there. I'm going to surprise my Uncle by introducing him before he gives the sermon today."

"Wow, that must be an honor. Giving the introduction, I mean."

"It certainly is. I can't wait to see how honored he's going to be."

"Oh, okay." My mind starts to wander.

People are piling in now. Bumping into both of us. He seems to become annoyed.

"Hey, I would like to chat with you some more, can I speak to you after service? I gotta get in there. My name is Elliot Nolan, by the way. What's yours?"

All giddy-eyed. I felt myself blushing. I finally say, "Ra yna... but everyone calls me *'Ray-Ray'*."

"Okay, Rayna. I will talk to you later." He walks through the foyer and the large double doors heading straight for the front pew near the Deacons' corner. He sits down and looks around. Still seemingly annoyed.

"Hey Ray-Ray, you going in or what!"

"Hey, Sierra! We have got to talk after service, girl!"

We finally walk in and take seats towards the front of the church because our usual seats closer to the middle are taken.

Oh my goodness! He is within my view! His smooth, clean-shaven face looks tight. "What's going on with him?" I wonder. "Lord, Elliot seems so well put together." I thought.

"Girl, where's your mind at? You daydreaming again?" Sierra nudges me. "Who are you staring at?"

"It's nothing, girl. You know me. *After* service, remember?"

"Praise God from whom all blessings flow!" shouts Pastor Johnson from the pulpit. "We are excited to have Pastor James Nolan, Sr. from *House of Prayer Missionary Baptist Church* visiting with us. He will be our speaker for today.

Before he comes and the choir sings, Pastor Nolan's nephew, Brother Elliot Nolan will come to introduce him. Let's give him a round of applause."

Panicky. Pastor Nolan looks up as if he's seen a ghost. He hadn't seen Elliot since that tragic night of Elijah's death!

Elliot who seemed to be reluctant to do the introduction, pulled a piece of paper from the inside pocket of his grey *Armani* suitcoat and walked to the podium our church Secretary uses to do the announcements. He fixed the mic, looked around the church, smiled at me, and began.

"Good morning, everyone. I am happy to introduce this awesome man of God to those who know and may not know him. He has suffered great losses yet still serves God. He was a devoted husband to his loving wife, Aunt Trudie who accidentally drowned in their backyard pool. The proud father of deceased children Kayla, Kristen, and James Nolan, Jr., all died in a house fire due to a gas explosion. I love serving the Lord because of my uncle's resilience. He taught me a lot about scriptures and how to apply them to my life. My favorite is Romans 12:19 "For vengeance is mine, I will repay, says the Lord." God's Word is so true. Please prepare your minds and hearts to hear the Word of God from this great man of God, my Uncle, Pastor James Nolan, Sr."

Everyone stands up and claps; surprisingly, even me. We all wanted to hug poor Pastor Nolan because of all his familial losses. Some of the mothers of the church wiped their teary eyes.

"What in the world?" says Sierra, "What's gotten into you? You're acting weird today! You know full well you never stand up! We're talking after service."

"Gimme a break, Sierra! It was a great introduction!"

"Yeah right. It ain't like that's the first introduction you heard from someone before."

I rolled my eyes and sat down glancing at Elliot who suddenly looked back. Our eyes locked on each other. I quickly grabbed my purse and started looking for a piece of gum. When I looked up, he was facing forward and clapping as the choir sang *Hezekiah Walker's,* "*Lord Lift Me Up.*" In my peripheral vision, I could see Sierra staring at me with that "private eye" investigative look.

"What time is it, church?" bellowed Pastor Johnson.

"Preaching time!" we shouted back. Well, most of us anyway. I couldn't keep my eyes off Elliot. His mouth didn't move. He was staring at his Uncle. His face was tight again.

Pastor Nolan walks slowly to the pulpit and says, "Friends, I have made so many regretful mistakes in my lifetime. I want you to know that God forgives and heals all wounds and the brokenhearted. I may have lost my loved ones but thank God that HE didn't allow me to lose my mind; however, I will be taking a leave of absence for a year starting in a few weeks. So please pray for and with me."

Everyone stands and claps. Some shouting out, "Hallelujah! Praise Jesus!"

Pastor Nolan continues, "My subject today is, 'God Loves and Forgives, No Matter What You've Done!' I will be coming from a familiar scripture: John 3:16. Everyone please stand, if you can, and let's read the scripture together."

Elliot remains seated. His jaws clenched tight.

"Why is he still sitting there?" I wondered. "What is his problem?"

The sermon was awesome! Pastor Nolan was a dynamic speaker. I was up and down off my seat several times witnessing to the Word. Sierra was so distracted by my actions, she could not focus. She kept nudging me and saying, "What has gotten into you!?"

Elliot did clap to witness the Word a couple of times.

We glanced at each other a few times. I felt nervous once the sermon was over. I remembered Elliot wanted to speak with me after service.

"You okay?" Sierra asks.

"Uh, yeah," I said hesitantly.

"You know, you've been acting weird throughout the entire service. I see you keep staring at that guy who gave the intro. What's up with that?"

"Nothing girl. I mean..."

"Don't gimme that *nothing* mess. We've been best friends since 4th grade. I know something's up. We'll talk later."

Just then, I heard Pastor Nolan say, "Repeat after me: May the Lord watch between me and thee while we're absent one from another. Amen, Amen, and Amen!"

Oh no, the benediction! I felt sick. My knees were weak. I no longer wanted to speak to Elliot. Why was I so nervous about talking to this guy? Sierra and I made our way outside near her red convertible Chevrolet Camaro Z28.

"Hi, beautiful lady!" A voice comes from out of nowhere. I'm speechless! It's Elliot!

"Well, hello. And who might you be?" Sierra butts in.

"Excuse me but I was talking to the beautiful Rayna." Elliot gives Sierra that 'mind your business' look.

"Well, excuse me but, I am talking to you." Sierra rolls her eyes at him and says, "Ray-Ray, how you know this fool!"

"Sierra! We are at church, remember? The scripture says, 'Keep your foot in the house of God', girl!"

Now Elliot butts in, "I'm not trying to be rude, but Rayna can I speak to you alone please?"

"Okay. Sierra, I will call you later. Love you, girl." Sierra looked at Elliot and rolled her eyes again. She gave me that *you betta call me* look and walked off.

"Your girl seems to have some serious issues. But I'm not going to waste time being annoyed by her problems. I want to get to know you. Here is my number." Elliot says and takes my phone.

"Excuse me! And you say Sierra has problems?" I snatch my phone back.

"Hey I was trying to give you my number but if you don't want it, I mean, I can move on."

"I **do** want your number. I just don't appreciate you grabbing my phone like that. Now, what's your number?"

He hesitates. "You know you're even prettier when you get upset!"

I began to smile forgetting about being agitated by the phone ordeal. He gives me his number.

"So when are you going to call me? Tonight at 8:00 sharp. I hope."

"I'll try to. If I'm not too busy."

"What you mean, *'too busy'*?"

"Well, it's Sunday, and I prepare my meals for the week, go to the park for ice cream with Grandma, call Sierra, and..."

"Hold up. It seems you may not be interested in getting to know me. Are you seeing someone already?"

"I have a friend but we're not in a *'real'* relationship; it's plutonic. Nothing serious."

"Well, Rayna...I'm interested in you...so, you need to dump that *friend*."

"Why?"

"Well, for starters...you have that *'sweet girl'* vibe...you're a *'church girl'*...I'm handsome and you're very attractive, and I'm better than him. Is that reason enough for you?"

I'm flattered and infatuated by his charming personality.

I see Grandma coming my way. She says, "Ray Ray! I'm going to eat dinner with Hilda Mae today. We going to Big Jim's Bar-B-Que. You wanna meet us there?"

"No, Grandma. I'm going to prepare my meals for the week, remember?"

"Oh, chile, I forgot. We can still go get ice cream at the park. Will you be done by 6:30?"

Elliot's jaws tightened.

"Yes, Grandma I will be finished."

"Hey, ain't you the young man that introduced your daddy, Pastor Nolan? You did a wonderful job!"

"It's my Uncle, not my Daddy, and yes ma'am my name is Elliot."

"Sorry, I didn't mean to offend you."

"All right, Florence you ready? Aunt Hilda Mae yelled across the parking lot.

"Hey, Aunt Hilda. Love you!"

"Love you too, Ray-Ray!"

Grandma Flo hugged me. "See you for ice cream. Nice to meet you, Elliot."

Grandma strutted across the parking lot and got in Aunt Hilda Mae's black Cadillac Escalade that she bought after she retired from teaching elementary school for 30 years.

Elliot turned to me and said, "I see you didn't introduce me to your grandmother. If you're not interested, then please tell me now. I don't like it when

people get my hopes up."

"I'm interested **man**. Relax!" I say jokingly. "And, no offense but ice cream at the park after Sunday Service is a family tradition; especially since Grandpa Harry died. Okay?"

"Whatever. Call me at 8:00 sharp tonight then." He gently kissed my hand and walked away.

I watched him as he strolled away with some pep in his step. He seemed so confident. Casual. Cool. I think he knows I'm staring. He got into a gold-colored Lexus convertible.

"That brutha is so well put together!" I thought. "And fine as wine, too!"

CHAPTER 6

WARNING SIGNS

Grandma and I met promptly at the park at 6:30. She explained that Mama didn't feel like coming today. She gets like that sometimes. I felt a little worried. I hoped she was okay. I said a silent prayer for her.

"Did you get your meals prepared for the week, baby?"

"I sure did, Grandma! Like clockwork!"

"Ray-Ray, Hilda Mae and I were talking about you and Pastor Nolan's nephew at dinner. You know you ain't but 22 and too young to get serious with anyone right now. It's all right to have associates but you let God send you Mr. Right because 'wrong' can come from anywhere through anyone. Deception is real Ray-Ray. Proceed with caution that's all we are saying. You are a smart girl. Wear your antennae and your cross. And keep your panties on!"

"Ah, c'mon Grandma. Give me some credit. I just met the man today and y'all act as if I'm getting married to him tomorrow!"

She sensed that I was a little agitated.

"I'm sorry baby. You know we want what's best for you that's all. You're so young. I saw the way you were both eyeing each other. I trust your judgment, Ray-Ray. Just pray, sweetie, before entering that door called "love."

"Seriously, Grandma. No worries." I hugged her to reassure her I wasn't upset with her. "What are you going to get today Grandma?"

"Your Granddaddy's favorite...a banana split with strawberries, pecans, whipped cream, topped with a cherry, and dripping with maple syrup."

I normally get two scoops of strawberry and vanilla topped with walnuts and chocolate syrup in a waffle cone bowl. We ate our ice cream while walking one lap around the park. She continued to give her and Aunt Hilda Mae's unwelcomed advice as I pretended to listen.

I arrived from the park at 7:30, washed my hands, and called Sierra before I got ready to settle in. "Thank God I don't work tonight. It's been a long day."

"Hey girl, I was wondering if he had stopped you from calling me."

"C'mon Sierra. It's not like that!"

"He's trouble, bestie. Something about him irks me. I think he's arrogant, jealous, and controlling."

"You can tell all that by interacting with him one time?"

"I didn't get my Doctorate at Chicago State University for nothing. Did you forget I'm a clinical psychologist now?"

"That's not fair, Sierra. You shouldn't go around analyzing people outside of work; especially without their permission?"

"Okay calm down. But you know we're always going to look out for one another."

"Everyone needs to stop treating me as though I can't think for myself. This is not a repeat of Mama and Daddy, you know."

"I know. I'm sorry. So have you talked to him since we left church yet?"

"No, I'm going to call him at 8:00." "Well, you only have ten minutes."

"No rush. It's not that serious."

Sierra and I began talking about everything; like we always do. That's my girl. There's nothing we can't share. No matter how embarrassing or hurtful.

"Uh-oh! *Somebody's* going to be in trouble," says Sierra.

"Girl, please!"

"Well, call me tomorrow. Love you."

"Okay, love you too, girl."

After I hung up, I didn't realize the time was now 8:15. I decided to go to the bathroom first and then call him. The phone rings three times. No answer. Fourth ring. No answer. I hung up. He finally calls around 9:00.

"Hi, Elliot."

"I thought I clearly said 8:00."

"Excuse me! I don't think I like your tone."

"I'm sorry. I don't like getting my hopes up."

"Look, we are both adults here. We have already been raised by..."

"Let me stop you right there. I wasn't raised by my parents. See, if you'd take the time to get to know me, then you wouldn't make that statement *smart mouth*."

"I apologize. My bad. But had you let me finish my statement, then you would find that I wasn't completely raised by mine either." I felt annoyed. "You know what? There's too much miscommunication between us. Maybe this isn't such a good idea."

"Rayna, wait. I'm sorry. Can we do our meet and greet over, please? I want to get to know you."

"Well, I guess," I said reluctantly.

"Let's have dinner at my place Wednesday night. I will cook for you."

"Uh, that's a no. I have to work. This girl is a 'night owl'. I'm a registered nurse at the hospital in the pediatric unit from 11 to 7."

"Can't you come around 8 and then go to work from here?"

"I'm afraid not. I have to get my beauty sleep." I burst out laughing.

"What's so funny? I'm serious. You pick a time and date then."

"Sure. I'm off Friday. We can meet for lunch at that new Mexican restaurant on the corner of Maple and Bay Street. I believe it's La Fiesta! How does that sound?"

"Meet? Why can't we ride together? You don't wanna be seen riding around town with me?"

"Why do you have to turn things around? Like your feelings always hurt about something? You okay?"

"What do you mean by that? What are you trying to say?"

"How are we going to get to know each other if we keep starting off on the wrong foot? You are *too* easily offended. I don't understand."

"I'm sorry. You're right. What time would you like to meet then?"

Something within me is screaming, **"Leave him alone!"**

But I ignore that still small voice and say, "12:30. We can meet at 12:30. You don't mind Mexican food do you?"

"I don't mind *stomaching* it. Chinese is my favorite though. But I will go to *La Fiesta!* as long as I get to spend time with you."

"All right, I look forward to seeing you Friday at 12:30 then."

"So does that mean we are not going to talk over the phone in the meantime?"

I rolled my eyes and started feeling annoyed again. "He seems a little clingy...a little needy." I think to myself.

"Hello? Am I talking to myself now?" he says.

"No, I'm here. I go to the gym from 7:15-8:15; come home and nap from 8:30-11:00; and before going to work, I sleep from 4 to 9. When I get up, I do a 30- minute workout, shower, and get ready for work."

"So, when is a good time to call you before you..., um, 'rest'?"

"Well, anytime between 11:30 and 3:30; otherwise, I will not answer. I believe in 'self-care'. I have to be ready for my little "peeps" while keeping my beauty and mental health intact."

"Sounds like I have to make an appointment just to talk to you."

"It's not like that, Mr. Sensitive. You have a 4-hour time frame." I said jokingly.

"I'm not sensitive, just receptive."

"Same thing, smarty pants!"

We both laugh.

"I love your laughter, you should do it more often."

"I will as long as I'm talking to you," he says.

Awkward silence.

CHAPTER 7

ELLIOT NOLAN...AND FAMILY

Now 24 years old, Elliott recalled how it was when he and his brother first moved in with his Uncle and his family. It was a deplorable, grievous day.

"You get on my nerves, Elliot. Looking just like your Daddy. The only reason you're here is because they died in that stupid car crash. I never saw what your Mama saw in Wesley anyway. Go to your room after you eat!"

"What did I do this time?" Eight-year-old Elliot thinks to himself. He finishes his food and goes to his room. "Mommy and Dad, I miss you so much." He cried silently on his pillow.

Wesley and Elisa Nolan

Wesley and Elisa Nolan were college sweethearts and married right after. They were elated to have their firstborn son, Elijah David Nolan. Then two years later, they welcomed Elliot Wesley Nolan to the family.

Despite their age differences, the boys looked like twins. The couple was so in love. Always laughing, hugging, and kissing. Right in front of the boys. Elijah and Elliot often teased each other that they wouldn't be doing that when they got older.

"Too mushy!" Elijah would say.

"Yeah, too mushy!" Elliot mocked his brother. Oh, how Elliot adored his family; idolizing his brother. Elliot had to wear matching outfits like his

brother. Every toy or gift Elijah received, Elliot felt he had to have it as well. The parents loved how much Elliot copied his brother. On the one hand, Elijah felt annoyed by it; sometimes. On the other hand, he felt proud that Elliot was his little 'shadow.'

Wesley, an acclaimed, award-winning gospel singer, and author while Elisa was a reputable criminal lawyer in Kelton, North Carolina, made sure the boys had everything they needed. Including tutors and nannies.

They lived such a lavish lifestyle filled with love, joy, and happiness.

That Tragic Night

"Honey, hurry up we are going to be late for the ceremony!" Elisa yelled to Wesley.

"Coming, babe! Wesley said from the music studio.

Wesley ran upstairs to the bedroom where Elisa was putting on her diamond earrings and necklace with a chic, flowing black gown that hugged her size 6 small-framed body.

"Woo, Lord have mercy, Mrs. Nolan! You finer than wine, baby!"

"Man, will you get in there and put your tux on? I don't want to be late for this one. I can't believe you're nominated for a Stellar Award for 'Best Gospel Song of the Year-God's All Right Wit Me'! I love that jazzy vibe, honey!"

The boys were playing a video game in Elijah's room when they heard the phone ring in their parent's bedroom. Probably the babysitter. They thought.

"No, you and Trudie don't have to keep the boys tonight, James. The neighborhood babysitter is watching them. Thanks for offering though. We gotta

go, big bro. Talk to you later...Hey, wait. Let's get the kids together this weekend. Okay. Awesome! "

Elijah and Elliot looked at each other. Whew! They didn't like going to their Uncle James' house without one or both of their parents.

The twins, Kayla and Kristen, were always mean to them and James Jr. would hit Elliot and Elijah and tell his Dad that they were trying to double-team him. Their Dad would always take James Jr.'s side without listening to Elliot and Elijah's side of the story. This made them feel helpless and frustrated, and it only made their relationship with James Jr. worse.

"Hey babe, James and I are taking the kids to *Buffalo Lanes* on Saturday. You know how much they love bowling."

"Okay, maybe Trudie and I can go to a movie or have a spa day then. C'mon, slowpoke!"

"It's pouring down out there, Lisa. I'll be glad when the storm lets up."

The boys pile into the room and lay across their parents' bed.

"Mom, do you think y'all should go out in this weather?" Elijah asked with worry.

"Ah, it's fine lil buddy." She gives them both a hug to reassure them.

Hours went by after their parents left them. Joanne was getting worried because it was 1:00 in the morning. The boys couldn't sleep. It wasn't unusual for her to stay over because she enjoyed getting paid extra cash. Maybe they decided to go to a hotel after celebrating too much. Everyone thought.

Joanne tried calling them but did not get an answer. The boys called them and did not get an answer either. They were nervous and worried.

Boom! Boom! Boom! Around 6:30 a.m., loud knocks at the door. Joanne ran from the guest room and opened the door. We heard her scream, "Oh no!" The police and Uncle James were visibly shaken by her crying.

"Your parents were killed in a car crash! They nabbed the idiot who hit them. Some drunk druggie. You have to come with me, boys!" Uncle James said.

And just like that! The boys were handed over to him.

The next day after the funeral, the attorney read the will their Mom had written. It stated: "In the event of Wesley and Elisa's death, we do hereby grant legal guardianship until Elijah reaches twenty-one. James Sr. and Trudie receive monthly stipends for taking care of the boys. If anything happens to Elijah such as alcohol or substance abuse, long-term incarceration, lifelong illness, or death, then the legal guardians will continue receiving stipends until Elliot turns twenty-one."

The boys, aged 8 and 10, didn't care about anything but wanted their parents to come get them. They couldn't stop crying while holding each other.

CHAPTER 8

THIS PECULIAR SUNDAY

On my way to Grandma's for ice cream with the top down on the convertible! It's hot again today; a scorching 97 degrees!

As I entered the doorway, I noticed that Mama looked different today! Is Mama sober? I don't want to stare. I certainly can't ask her. I give her a big hug and kiss on the cheek. She doesn't smell like booze and weed.

"Hi, Mama! You look nice! You going with us for ice cream?"

"Yeah. I'll go for ice cream."

Whaaat? Mama going with us! Something's going on.

Lord, I believe prayer is working! I silently thank God by doing a little praise shuffle.

You're smiling a lil hard today baby girl. Who is he?"

"What are you talking bout, Mama? Ain't no "he."

"Chile, don't let Ms. Thang fool you! Grandma butts in. "That girl done met a hottie! Looks like he came from "*Chips and Dealers*"... You know them, strippers."

We laughed so hard. Mama asked Grandma what she knew about the strippers, "*Chip and Dale's*."

"Girl I ain't been saved all my life! I had fun during my college years!"

We all laughed again. I've never seen Mama laugh so much except when she and Daddy weren't fussing over drugs. Mama is so pretty. She looks like she's glowing today! "God, please deliver my Mama." I pray in my heart. Then my phone rang.

"What you want!"

"Have y'all left for ice cream yet?"

"Nope."

"Mind if I tag along?"

"Sure, come on over. You know the address. See you when you get here."

"Hmmm!" Mama laughed.

I love it! Mama's laughter. Her smile. I can't wait to ask Grandma about what's going on.

Boom! Boom! Boom! There's a knock at the door. "I'll get it!" I jumped up! Smiling on my way to the door.

"Hey Sierra, girl!"

I looked back at Mama and Grandma and burst out laughing as they were anticipating that it was "*he.*"

They both rolled their eyes and then laughed. Sierra was staring at us like a deer in headlights.

"Have y'all been drinking?" she asked.

"No, girl. I'm messing with these nosy foxes! They thought it was...*him!*"

"Oh, that fool!"

"Sierra!" I scoffed at her.

"I don't know what you trying to be so secretive for. And we ain't **nosy**, just concerned." Grandma shouted from the kitchen.

"Yes, ma'am Grandma. Love you, love you, love you!"

Mama suddenly looked distant. Her thoughts seemed miles away. Daydreaming.

"You okay, Mama?" I asked.

She didn't answer. I looked at Grandma. I felt nervous.

"Earth to Carol!" Grandma cried out. She took her daughter by the hands.

Mama jumped. And so did I. "Mama, what's wrong?" I started crying.

She immediately stood up and hugged me. "Hush baby girl. I'm all right. I was just wondering about your Daddy that's all. Don't cry. I'm going to be fine. You will see."

"Mama, what's going on with you?"

Sierra gives me some tissue to dry my eyes and sniffles. "Well, baby girl, I've decided to check myself into Sumnerfield's Recovery and Rehabilitation Center for Addicts. I will be in there for a year. I go in tomorrow."

Grandma smiled as if she already knew. Sierra and I looked at each other. I was partially in disbelief and amazement. We all ran over to Mama and gave her a big hug.

Sierra smiled and said, "I set it up for her. But she is the one who came to ask me, Ray-Ray. I'm happy for you Mama C. I will do all I can to help. You've already made the first step and my Mama always says 'God will make two'."

"Oh goodness, this does call for a celebration! Let's go get some ice cream and you can tell me all about it!"

My thoughts start running in my head. "Why was Mama thinking about Daddy?" "Does she miss him?"

This is one peculiar Sunday!

CHAPTER 9

ANOTHER TRAGIC NIGHT

Since their parents' deaths, Elliot relied and depended on Elijah all the more. When their Uncle James would give them chores, Elliot would always check with Elijah first. This upset Uncle James and he would discipline Elliot to remind him that "You are a child and you will do as a child." He never hit Elijah; only Elliot.

On Elijah's sixteenth birthday, he planned to run away and take Elliot with him. He had befriended the quarterback on the team who said they could live with them because his parents were away on business trips most of the time. Drake Hudson, the Senior QB, was seventeen and stayed home alone. He was an ESPN Top 100 prospect and committed to the Tennessee University Bulldogs.

As they had packed their belongings in suitcases and duffle bags, James Jr., also 16, saw what they were doing. He said he wanted to go too or he would tell. He and Elijah started arguing. Then fighting. It spilled over into the hallway. When Uncle James, Aunt Trudie, and the twins came sprinting out of their bedrooms, they began screaming at Elijah to get off their son; their brother.

Elijah and James Jr. kept fighting until they were breaking furniture. Elliot was crying and pleading with Elijah to stop so they could leave.

"What do you mean leave? Neither of you is going anywhere?"

The fighting ensued as Elijah began strangling James Jr. Each of their faces and knuckles was bloody with cuts and bruises. Everyone was looking on in horror, as Uncle James went and got his black, leather belt from one of the kitchen drawers. "You will be struck with the '*rod of correction*' to drive out your foolishness, boy. That's what the Word says. Now get off my son!"

Elijah's ears were deafened by James Jr.'s gurgles, and he hadn't heard his uncle's voice. Uncle James brutally struck him with one blow to the head. For the first time, he hit Elijah! Elliot jumped on his uncle's back to stop him. But his Uncle was much bigger; more powerful, and threw Elliot to the floor. James Jr. was lying on the floor seemingly unconscious; barely breathing. Aunt Trudie and the twins leaning over him crying uncontrollably.

Elliot was sobbing profusely and plummeted to the floor. Elijah's face was bloody now; drip! drop! Beads of blood trickling down his face to his neck from his head. His limp body just lying there. Hands still. Not moving. "Elijah, Elijah!" Elliot screams. He lays across Elijah, "Don't leave me, brother. You can't go! C'mon, we have to leave! I need you! Elijah get up! Mom! Dad! where are you?" Please, God, don't take my brother!"

"Call 9-1-1 Trudie and tell them how Elijah attacked James Jr. and he's unconscious. We need an ambulance right away."

"Liars! You're all liars! You will have your part in the lake! My lake! You will each get yours." Elliot knelt by Elijah kissed and hugged him, and whispered, "Don't worry brother. I will avenge you. I promise!"

When the police and paramedics arrived, Elijah was pronounced dead at the scene and James Jr. was rushed to the hospital. The police did not charge James Sr. with murder.

Child Protective Services took Elliot into foster care after Uncle James requested they remove him from the home.

Chapter 10

OUR FIRST DATE

It's been such a hectic week at work. We lost a little one—stillbirth. I can still hear that wailing mother and father. I hope and pray I never experience that type of pregnancy. Nor a miscarriage. I don't think I could handle it.

My phone has been ringing all day. I told Elliot I would call him back around noon since it's my day off. I had been crying all morning as I thought about that young woman who lost her baby this week. She wasn't that much older than me. Around twenty-five. It was a little girl.

I guess I better answer this phone. "Hello!"

"What's your problem?" Elliot said angrily, "If you don't want to go tonight, then just say *so*! Dang!"

"Listen, I've had a rough week. It might be best if we change our date to Sunday when I'm off again. Maybe I'll feel better then."

"Hey, wait. I'm sorry. How bout I come over and you can tell me all about it? Please, I really wanna see you."

"Okay, but I don't feel like going out anywhere." "No problem. Can I cook for you?"

I was hesitant. "Uh, let's just order something from Uber Eats or Door Dash."

"That's fine. But I *can* cook."

I ignored the latter statement and said, "I will see you at 6:00. Okay?"

"Why so late? I mean, ain't you off today?" Elliot sounded frustrated.

"Look, Mr. Sensitive...!"

"Wait, girl! Please don't refer to me as *Mr. Sensitive*!"

"Well, stop acting like it. See you at 6:00 if **you** are still interested. I have to go now."

"Fine then! See you at six, Ms. Rude."

I hung up.

Elliot's face tightened, and he threw his phone across the bed nearly landing on the floor. While staring at himself in the mirror, he says, "I see I'm going to have to teach her a lesson sooner or later! She's too mouthy and defiant."

I took a shower and quickly went by *Stacy's Boutique* to buy myself a new outfit. I called Sierra and told her what happened as I was eyeing a bright red knee-length sleeveless dress. "Too naughty!" I think.

"Girl get rid of that fool! I'm telling you he ain't right. Something wrong with him."

"I know what I'm doing, sis. He's a little sensitive but harmless."

"If you say so. Remember, if you play around the fire, you're likely to get burnt."

"All right Mother Hen! I laugh. "Stop being such a 'Debbie Downer' and be happy for me."

"Look, girl, you are my closest friend. I love you!"

I make my way to the counter to purchase that 'naughty' red dress. "I love you too! I will call you tomorrow."

"You betta!"

I go to the nearest supermarket and pick up some snacks, wine, water, and beer. I don't even know what he likes or wants. "Well, *Mr. Sensitive,* you can eat it or leave it; drink it or dump it."

On my way to get gas after leaving the supermarket, the phone rings.

"Yes?"

"Hey beautiful, I can't wait to see you in a few minutes."

"Yeah, me too! I picked up a few things from the super-market."

"I thought we were going to order out."

"We are. Look, I'm almost home and have to get ready."

"Where you at? Where have you been?"

"Mr. Nosy, if you must know. I went shopping, to the supermarket, and to get gas."

We both started laughing.

I finally made it home. I forgot how busy Fridays are around town.

"Girl, you are looking mighty fine in that red dress!" Elliot said when I opened the door.

He had a velvety black wine bag with a red ribbon wrapped around it in his hand.

"You're looking *cute,* yourself! I like that red shirt you're wearing. What a coincidence."

"Who are you calling *cute*!? You know I'm finer than this wine!"

"Ain't a little arrogant are you?"

"Nah, I just don't have low self-esteem."

"Touché, oh fine one," I say sarcastically. "So what do you want to eat, my beauty."

"How about some seafood from *Katie's Crab Shack*?"

"Or, my Queen, some Chinese from Great Taste of China." Elliot interrupted abruptly.

"Now how are you going to ask me what I want to eat, then you make the decision," I say jokingly.

"You're right, beautiful. My bad." He leans over to kiss me on my cheek.

Wow! Such soft, sensuous lips. I feel tingly and light. "You, okay, beautiful?"

"Sure! Um, We can eat Chinese. Will you put in the order while I pour us each a glass of wine?"

"Yeah, pour the wine I brought, please. You will find it rather tasteful."

"Certainly, my lord! I look at him and smile. I love his beautiful green-brown eyes. So dreamy; yet mysterious.

He made the call swiftly and said it should arrive in fifteen to twenty minutes. He makes his way to the couch and motions for me to sit next to him as I bring over the drinks.

"A toast to such a beautiful lady that I can't wait to have the honor of knowing better."

Clink! We drink up. Talking mostly about our families.

I tell him about my mom and dad's drug addiction how my dad left Sumnerfield when I was six and my mom's sudden resolve to enter rehab.

Elliot tells of being eight years old when he was raised by his Uncle James and Aunt Trudie in Kelton, North Carolina. His mom and dad were killed in a car crash by some drunken drug addict. He teared up as he spoke of them. How much he adored them.

I felt the urge to hug him; hold him; comfort him. "Oh, baby, that's horrible! I try to sympathize with

him, "Looks like we both suffered some traumatic childhood experiences."

"Yeah, but mine was worse than yours, Rayna!" he yells, "You got to have a better childhood with your grandparents." He balls up his fists and stares at me.

I got scared and backed away from him.

"Why are you looking at me like that?" He's coming towards me now. His eyes are so distant.

I look down at his tightly, clenched fists.

He stops and looks at his hands and unclenches them; then reaches out to hug me.

I flinched and started to cry.

"I will never hurt you beautiful. I just get so worked up talking about it." He fell to his knees pleading with me to stop crying.

Then as our eyes met, our bodies gently caressed each other as we kissed. Such soft, sensuous lips. He dries my salty tears with his tender kisses. My body was on fire!

My loins were hot with desire. I wanted more! He starts sweating as his lips kiss my neck and ease to my plump, perky breasts. Gently teasing each hardened nipple.

Ding! Dong! Ding! Dong!

Woo! Saved by the bell! I thought.

We're both startled and immediately separated as two young teenagers who got caught by their parents. We laugh and he answers the door.

"The food smells delicious!" he says, "but not as much as you do!"

He set the plates on the espresso kitchen island with the cream-colored granite top. He walks over and grabs me by my tiny waist, thrust me onto the couch, and passionately kisses me all over while ripping my dress off.

"I just bought this dress!" I thought.

His hands and mouth were all over me. I no longer cared. I could not control my body or my thoughts. We proceeded with the breathtaking consummation like two wild animals in heat. We didn't even make it to the bedroom!

Really? On my white deluxe plush carpet on the living room floor?

I didn't even think about it being our first date!

CHAPTER 11

"IS THAT YOU, DADDY?"

I can't wait to call Sierra! What a night of passionate lovemaking! I've never made love three times in a
night! My thighs and legs are sore. My neck and breasts
are bruised with hickeys. I was tossed and turned so
much. I still feel dizzy. I can't wait to see Elliot again!

I call Sierra and tell her about it! She chastises me for
"giving away my cookies" on the first date. I tell her I
couldn't help myself. It's like I was magnetized; hypno-
tized.

"Are you sure he didn't slip a Mickey in your drink?"

"No girl! Why do you have to spoil it for me?" I walk
over to the window and peep through my blind to look
at people walking and eating at the park.

"Sierra, I have to call you back!" I hang up immediately
and quickly slip on a pair of gym shorts and a tee shirt.
I don't know if I'm matching. I don't care. It can't be! I
sprint to the park as though I'm running the 100- yard
dash. I'm almost out of breath.

"Excuse me, Sir."

The gentleman slowly turns around. He looks at me
with familiar eyes and smiles at me.

"Daddy? Is it you?"

The gentleman replies, "Uh, no miss. I don't have any children. But thank you."

He walks on. I'm left standing there with an 'egg on my face'. I feel so embarrassed.

I go to Grandma Flo's and tell her about what happened. She's busy cooking a small dinner of lasagna with a salad, and garlic bread.

"You wanna stay for dinner? I have enough for four."

"Sure." I start pacing in the kitchen around the table. "I miss Daddy, Grandma." I start crying frantically.

Grandma rushes over to hug me. "Oh honey," she says, "I knew this was bound to happen. You haven't seen him in so many years. Of course, you miss him. Why don't you try to find him? Did he ever write to you?"

She hands me some Kleenex and motions for me to sit down.

"I haven't heard from him since...that day in the park. He said he couldn't stay in Sumnerfield anymore because he wanted to get better."

"Okay here's what we'll do. We will hire David Barbour, one of your Granddaddy's friends who retired from the police force. He's a private eye now. I know he can find your Daddy."

"Thanks, Grandma."

"All right, let's eat! Remember, Romans 8:28 says: *"All things work together for the good of them that love God..."*

"Yes ma'am."

Grandma eats and calls him.

"Thanks for getting right on it, David. Don't forget, his name is *Raymond Anthony Brown*. I appreciate it.

Yeah, I miss him too. I'll talk to you later. Bye." And she hangs up. "David's going to check it out Ray-Ray. We should know something by tomorrow."

"Tomorrow?"

"Yep, I told you he would get to it."

"Hallelujah! Praise Jesus!" I throw up my hands and do my praise shuffle.

"That's the praise I wanna see...but more of it down at the church."

"Yes ma'am, Grandma. Love you, love you, love you! Bye. Thanks for dinner!"

I couldn't sleep a wink. I only thought of Daddy. What does he look like now? I wondered. Is he still pecan tan, handsome, small build, tall, and has his dreadlocks? If he saw me now, would he recognize me? I didn't recognize him. Mistaken identity at the park.

"I miss you, Daddy," I whispered.

I woke up to thunder and lightning the next morning.

It was raining so hard. The phone rang. I ran to get it off the charger. Is it Grandma with news about Daddy? I wondered with excitement. I stubbed my toe on the bed. "Dang, it!"

Oh, it's Elliot!

"Hi, Elliot! I think my smile reached Heaven when I heard his voice.

"Hi, beautiful lady!"

"I'm getting ready to head to the gym. I just got off, remember?"

"I know Ms. Rude," he said chuckling, "I was wondering if I could meet you there. I could use a *workout*. If you know what I mean."

"I sure could too! See you there."

Here we go again! The best morning consummation ever! Right there in the locker room. Enjoyed this workout! Better than any treadmill, punching bag, or weightlifting. You name it. We worked off a lot of energy and steam. We kissed goodbye and went to our separate dwellings. I can't believe we didn't get caught! I hope there were no cameras. I didn't even care. Am I in love? or is this lust? I've gotta talk to Mama and Grandma!

As soon as I pull into the driveway, my phone is blowing up. Before I pick up, I think, "Elliot must miss me already." There's that smile reaching Heaven! I didn't look to see who was calling.

"Hey, baby! Miss me already?"

"Uh, yeah!" Grandma disguised her voice.

"Not funny, Grandma! I was embarrassed and tried to laugh it off.

"Hey Ray-Ray, he found your Daddy! David found him!"

I feel faint. I can't breathe. I can't speak.

"Ray-Ray? You there? Did you hear what I said, baby?"

"I-I-I don't believe it, Grandma. He's alive! Is he okay?" I'm shaking with excitement and fear.

"Yes, he's alive and well! Come over and I will tell you all about it."

I know I'm supposed to lie down now because I worked a 12-hour shift last night. My adrenaline is rushing so fast that I don't feel tired at all. I stopped by Café Joe's to pick up two mocha espressos.

When I arrived, Grandma was already sitting on the porch. Her smile touching Heaven! We embraced and jumped up and down with excitement.

"Here's the number you can reach him at Ray-Ray! Go call him!"

"What do I say, Grandma? I haven't seen or heard from him for over eight, almost nine years." I started crying and buried my head in Grandma Flo's chest which smelled like she just finished cooking bacon and eggs.

She stroked my hair as if I was ten again.

"C'mon Ray. You've wanted to talk to him since the day he left. I know you love him. Words will come to you. God will give you what to say; you just open up your mouth."

"That's easy for you to say."

"Well, here's the number. The ball's in your court, Ray-Ray."

I felt like talking to Elliot. I wanted his opinion. I called him and told him what was going on.

"Are you kidding, Rayna? I envy you. Your parents are alive. I would give anything to be able to talk to my parents again. To hug them. To tell them how much I love them. You're selfish, Rayna! Spoiled and selfish!" He hung up the phone. He was angry.

I started bawling. I called him back immediately. He didn't pick up.

"Maybe I am 'spoiled and selfish'." I thought.

I called him again. No answer. I left a message. I begged and pleaded for him to call me back. "I'm sorry Elliot. Please call me! You're right. Maybe I am 'spoiled and selfish'."

I took a shower and wailed the whole time.

The phone rang as I was getting out of the shower. "Hey, beautiful," he said calmly, "I'm sorry for calling you 'spoiled and selfish'. I love you, Rayna!"

"What? You love me?"

"Yeah! You my beautiful girl."

"I love you too, Elliot!"

"Beautiful, I hope you know what you're saying."

"I love you, I love you, I love you."

There's a knock at the door.

"Say it again beautiful!"

"I love you, Elliot!" We sealed it with another day of wild passion...showered together, and then Elliot said, "Call your Daddy. I wish I could call mine." His face was tight again. He got dressed; and then left.

I was getting ready to lie down before my night shift, when I searched my pocket to find the piece of paper Grandma handed me with the number on it. I nervously punched in the digits on the keypad. The phone rang.

My hands were shaking. There was a woman's voice on the other end.

At once, I hung up the phone.

Straight away, my phone rang back.   Reluctantly, I answered.

"Hello?" The man said.

I was numb; paralyzed by fear. It sounds like Daddy!

"Hello? May I ask who called my wife earlier? She seems to be upset."

Oh, it's him! I hope. No, I know it!

"Is that you, Daddy?" My voice was shaking. Then I started crying.

"Ray-Ray!"

I hung up. I'm not ready.

CHAPTER 12

HERE'S TO SOBRIETY

"Calm down, Carol! You've got to calm down!" Dr. Jennifer Kysinsky told her.

Carol was screaming and scratching herself...mainly her arms and legs. She was balled up like a ball of yarn. Clawing at the sheets. Yelling at everyone. Delusional. Hallucinations.

The two male orderly nurses strapped her to the bed so that Dr. Kysinsky could give her a shot to calm her nerves.

"That's right, relax. It's withdrawals that's all. You're going to be fine."

Carol finally went to sleep and was taken to a padded room to make sure she did not harm herself or others.

Some days seemed worse than others. There were days that she cried, vomited, refused to talk to anyone, and fought everyone who came near her to give her a shot or medicine. Back in the straps.

This went on for a few weeks until the medications started taking effect. Carol was diagnosed with schizophrenia, anxiety, and depression; yet she would not attend the therapy sessions. She was too ashamed; overwhelmed.

"It's okay," Counselor Troy always says, "she will join when she's ready. When she's comfortable."

Carol sat in her room and read the Bible that she received from her Mama. She loved that it talked about forgiveness of sins, forgiving others, and yourself. She felt that was hard to do, but the more she read it, the better she felt about herself.

One day she decided to attend a therapy session to listen to the others. That one day soon turned into more days. Sometimes she would cry. No one judged her.

Some would cry with her. They felt each other's hurt; each one's pain as they spoke about their tragedies; their wrongs; their regrets.

Carol looked at each person around the room. She started to realize that "I'm not the only one who feels guilty or ashamed. I'm not the only one who is desperately wanting to change; to live again. I can do this. I must. I want to live!"

She quickly stood up and walked briskly to the podium and said, "Hi, my name is Carol, and I'm a drug addict. It's been 125 days since my sobriety. I haven't wanted to be a part of the group because I'm ashamed of

the hurt I caused my family. I left my little girl alone to get high when she was only ten and the State took her from me and gave her to my Mama and Daddy.

I feel guilty every time I think about what could have happened to her while she was left alone. You see, we lived on the rough side of town and anything could've happened to her. Raped, trafficked, drugged...Oh, God!"

Carol begins to cry uncontrollably and falls to the floor. Counselor Troy consoles her and ends the session. The fifteen others in the group look on in sorrow with tear-filled eyes.

Counselor Troy walks Carol back to her room. "You know, I'm glad Sierra referred you to me, Carol. It takes time but you're going to be fine. Please keep coming to therapy and release your internal fears, regrets, and wrongs. Don't hold back. Don't hold it in. Your mind cannot handle the pressure. Peace of mind is what you should seek. Your outer scars are healing nicely. Now let us work on those inner scars; your inner being. I'm so proud of you for speaking out today."

Carol was exhausted once she returned to her room.

The doctor gave her a shot of Haldol. Carol took a shower, read a few scriptures, and then went to sleep. Each day Carol continued going to therapy, taking her medications, and reading her Bible. She has never felt better. Occasionally, she would think about Raymond. "How is he?" she wondered. Then, she would shake her head. "That was moon's ago! He's probably moved on."

"Visiting day is coming up next week, Counselor Troy boasted, "You should all be proud. Remember, you've come so far but every day is a new day and a new beginning. You must not fret or worry about your sobriety. Only take one day at a time. Now, please fill out your visitor's form so we can have a head count for refreshments. Leave it at the front desk. Thank you."

"I can't wait to see my son!" A member of the group says to Carol. "Do you have someone special coming for the visit?" he asks.

"Yes. My mom and daughter." Carol says seeming to blush.

They both glance at each other and he says, "Here's to sobriety." He smiles and walks away.

Carol watches him with a smile on her face from Earth to Heaven.

CHAPTER 13

THE PROPOSAL

"Good morning beautiful. You okay?" he laughed. "Yeah, baby, I'm fine!" 'Baby?' Did I just call him 'baby'?

"So are you my girl or what?"

Something tells me to say, "No!" However, I think of that passionate night and quickly say, "Yes!"

"You don't know how happy you've made me. I feel on top of the world!" he yells.

"You sound like it! Happy to oblige! Can't wait to do it all over again."

"Oh, we will as soon as we get married."

"Wait, what? But you just asked me to be your girl-friend."

"Nope, I said 'Are you my girl? Meaning, *my wife*." "But we don't know each other that well. We've only been on a couple of dates and...!"

"I thought you said you love me." he sounds frustrated.

"Elliot, I do have feelings for you."

"Feelings? That's all! Girl, I told you "I love you! I don't just go around saying that to everyone. Not to anyone! He hangs up the phone.

I start crying again and call Sierra.

"Whoa! Slow down! What's wrong Ray-Ray?" "He wants me to marry him! He was upset with me
because I said I have feelings for him; that marriage is so soon."

"Girl, get rid of that fool! I told you something's not right about him. Why is he rushing the relationship?
Dang, Ray! What kinda cookies have you got?"

"This is not funny, Sierra. I'm so confused right now.
I do love him."

"Whaaaat? You don't even know him. Careful.
You're opening a door with a black hole that's going to suck you in."

"Hey Sierra, let me call you back. He's beeping in." "Elliot, I'm not saying I don't want to marry you.
Just wait."

"Look, Rayna can I come over please? Let's talk in person, please."

"Okay, I will see you when you get here."

I quickly showered, put on my black silk nighty, and tidied up the place. I put out a couple of champagne glasses with the wine on ice.

The doorbell rang. Running to the door, I stubbed my toe on the corner of the marble espresso coffee table. "Dang!" I whispered while limping to the door.

"Grandma!"

"Well, looks like I'm not *him*! You expecting company?"

"You couldn't call Grandma? It must be something important."

"It is. Your Mama wants us to come for a visit next week at the Center. She sounds happy Ray-Ray."

My face must be grimacing with pain. "What's wrong with you? Where are you hurting?"

"I'm fine, Grandma. I just stubbed my toe." "Broke or fractured it more like it, the way you're

reacting. Sit down. Where's your first-aid kit?"

The doorbell rang...again. I get up to answer it while Grandma is scrounging around in my bathroom to look for the kit.

"Hi, Elliot!" I said wincing in pain.

"Hey beautiful," he gently kisses me, "What's wrong? Are you hurt?" he picks me up and sits me on the chair just as Grandma is walking in.

"Well, aren't you quite the gentleman? Ray-Ray you betta keep him chile! Put your foot up here baby so I can wrap it."

"No offense, Ms. Flo but Rayna is my responsibility.

I will take care of her. Thank you for stopping by." "Well excuse me. I know when I'm not wanted,"

Grandma said laughing, "Just make sure you do it right! Ray-Ray I will check on you tomorrow and we will talk about the visit to see your Mama. Love you, sweetie."

"Okay, Grandma. Love you too!"

"Don't get up you two. I can see myself out."

Once she leaves, Elliot grabs me and starts kissing me all over. He rips off my nighty and passionately fills me with his love. My heart is pounding so hard as if it's going to burst through my chest.

"Oh, Elliot! I scream. My toe...writhing in pain.

He continues wildly, passionately, harder, faster, and faster. Beads of sweat rolling down his back...off his face onto mine. Suddenly, he stops!

I open my eyes. My body is so hot! "What's wrong? Please, don't stop!"

"Marry me, Rayna! I need you! I love you! We can have this every night!"

He begins again. I can't help myself. I feel a cold piece of metal on my finger as we are making love.

"Yes, yes, yes! Oh, yes, Elliot! I'll marry you!"

He picks me up and whisks me to the bedroom where we go on for another 30 minutes.

The air is filled with our love. Breathe in. Breath out.

As Elliot is holding me, I dizzily stare at my ring! I no longer feel the pain in my toe!

CHAPTER 14

MR. AND MRS. RAYMOND ANTHONY BROWN

"Honey who was that on the phone?" Tasha sounded concerned.

"My daughter, sweetie. I think I'm ready for a visit now. I have a lot of explaining to do."

"I agree. Can the kids and I go with you?"

"Not on the first visit. I need to tell her about you and them. I had a lot to think about while I was in that prison for 10 years. It truly was a blessing in disguise. I was finally able to get clean and sober. Thanks to God for allowing me to meet you."

"Do you remember when we met? You were so afraid of me."

"Well, you did have a gun strapped around you. Even though you were a nurse in the infirmary."

"Yeah, but it wasn't for you, honey. I felt calm around you. I wasn't nervous or afraid to talk to you. You didn't frighten me like the others. Your kind, remorseful eyes are what drew me to you. I knew you were a good man. I'm so glad I met and married you,
Ray!"

"Daddy, look at this car I put together!" a little 6- year-old boy said.

Raymond started crying. He remembered how he used to teach Ray-Ray to build model cars.

"What's wrong with Daddy, Mommy?"

"Anthony Ray, please go play so Daddy can get some rest. He will see your car later. Okay?"

"Okay, Mommy." He runs off to play with his little 6-year-old sister.

"Honey, did you take your Risperdol?"

"No, I didn't take it this morning or yesterday. I forgot."

"Ray! You have to take it, baby. Never mind, I will get it."

"Thanks, sweetie!"

"Hey, Daddy come play with us!"

"Okay, let me take my medicine first baby cakes." "Latisha Rae, please get your toys off the kitchen

floor. I almost stepped on them." "All right, Mommy. Coming!"

Raymond and Tasha both play with the twins before dinner. Afterwards, they eat and the kids take baths.

Once they're in bed, Tasha reminds Ray to take his medicine daily. He kisses her and tells her how grateful he is to have her in his life. When he falls off to sleep, Tasha sits up staring at him. She reminisces about how they met, fell in love, married, and had twins.

He was brought into the infirmary one night after attempting suicide from a terrible car accident he had caused. He was talking out of his mind. Screaming, "I'm sorry, I didn't see them! I didn't mean to hit them. I swear!"

His tormented body showed many cuts and bruises. He had used razors to cut himself and the wall and jail bars to beat up his frail body.

He was given a tranquilizer and soon drifted off to sleep mumbling, "I'm sorry, so sorry!"

For the next few days, he was in and out of consciousness. Sweating, twitching, crying, screaming, aching. Balled up in writhing pain. The doctor continued treatment for withdrawals and Nurse Tasha continued monitoring Raymond's vitals.

When he finally came to himself, he wanted to know where he was. Tasha told him he was in the Firth County State Prison infirmary.

"Infirmary?"

"Yeah, you've been here for about four months now.

They brought you in because you tried to commit suicide."

He began to cry. He wouldn't talk for days.

Finally, Tasha brought him a Bible to read and said, "Don't just open it, read it. This book will heal your mind and heart. It certainly will teach you to forgive yourself."

He wouldn't touch it. He turned over and stared at the wall thinking of Sumnerfield and how he had to leave Rayna behind.

Nurse Tasha kept hounding him to read the Bible. "All right, one scripture, lady! He says to her angrily.

The next thing he knew, he was reading it every day and giving her scriptures. For the next couple of weeks, as he got better, they started up a friendly chat.

"So how long have you been a nurse?"

"Over 15 years now. Right here in Kelton, North Carolina."

"You always worked in the prison?

"No, I was at Kelton Memorial Hospital where I met a man who had robbed a store. He had been shot and wasn't receiving proper medical care at the prison infirmary. I made up my mind I wanted to make a difference to help prisoners. They're people too regardless of what they've done. I've been working here at Firth for about 6 years now."

"Besides a nurse are you a minister as well?"

"Not by title or paper. According to the Bible, we all are witnesses for the Word of God."

"Okay, Ms. Thang," he said flirtingly with a smile to Heaven.

"How are you doing? With your thoughts, I mean.

She seemed concerned.

"I'm fine, I guess. I'm going to start therapy soon. I mean, I feel better with the medication but I know that church and therapy will help me be stable-minded. I think it can help me heal inside and out. I can't change what I did but I pray I can help someone else not do what I did. How long am I going to be in this infirmary?"

"Until the doctor releases you. You still have a long road to recovery. I wouldn't mind if you could pull your entire sentence here. You're a good soul, Raymond Anthony Brown. I can tell. You just made a big mistake and tried to take your own way out. God has given you a second chance at life."

"Well, thank you. Being sober makes it hard to face what I've done. I want a drink and to shoot up so bad, but I also want to get better. I'm glad it didn't work!"

"What?" Tasha asked with curiosity.

"My suicide. It feels good to talk with someone who doesn't seem to judge me."

"Oh, of course. You'll be fine as long as you change your environment and your circle."

"My circle?"

"Yeah, your circle of family and friends. You will need to remove anyone or anything from your circle that may hinder your sobriety. Think of a plant. It's not going to grow without the proper nutrients, air, light, soil, temperature, and water. You won't be able to grow unless you're surrounded by a strong support group with the same mindset, get therapy, and in a good church. It won't hurt to take medications either. If people can take

medication for high blood pressure, diabetes, and headaches, I don't know why they feel like they can't take medicine for mental illness. It's a sickness too, you know."

"You make a lot of sense. See, I need someone like you in my corner."

"I'm a supporter, not an enabler, honey. I sound sweet but am tough as nails."

As Tasha watched Raymond breathe in and out calmly and slowly, she was reminded of how she waited for him to serve his sentence. How they quietly and quickly fell in love upon meeting each other in the infirmary.

"Crazy!" All her family and friends told her. But Tasha always felt different about Raymond from day one. Now we are getting ready to celebrate 5 years of marriage soon! I feel he's my *'diamond in the ruff'*. He has a good soul who made a terrible mistake.

"I hope his daughter will be good for his circle," Tasha thought, "and what about her mother?"

She lay down next to her husband and whispered, "I love you, Ray!" in his ear, and went to sleep.

CHAPTER 15

ELLIOT'S NIGHTMARE

I'm so glad Elliot is spending the night! "Mrs. Elliot Nolan. No! Rayna Nolan!" I thought. I look at my ring one more time before drifting off to sleep.

"Stop! Get off him! Let's go, Elijah! We have to go!" Elliot yells.

I awake to a loud voice. "Elliot, baby, wake up." I shake him.

"You will pay. You all will have your part in my lake. Vengeance is mine! Noooo!"

He starts to cry. I continue to shake him. "Baby, wake up! What's wrong?"

"Get your hands off of me!" he screams at me. His eyes seem distant...as though he's someone else altogether.

"Elliot, you're scaring me, baby!" I start to cry.

"Hush up! You hear me!" He starts shaking me. I cry louder...harder.

"Elliot, stop!" I finally get free and run to the bathroom locking the door behind me. I think I scratched him.

Crying uncontrollably. I look at the ring. I don't want it anymore. My shoulders have small bruises caused by his tight grip on me.

"Rayna, open the door, please. I'm sorry. Give me a chance to explain. Open the door, please. I'm so sorry!" He starts crying.

I feel sorry for him. I open the door. We both hold each other. He kisses my hand and notices the ring is missing. He stops crying.

"Where's your ring?"

"In the bathroom on the sink. I took it off because I was afraid of you. You were shaking me and now I have bruises on my shoulders."

"What? I would never hurt you. I'm sorry for frightening you. You know I wouldn't intentionally do it," he lets her go, "If you don't want to marry me, I'll leave and never bother you again." He gets up to get dressed but I grab him and hug him. I hold on tight.

"Don't go, baby!" I get the ring and put it back on. "Baby, tell me about the nightmare. Who's Elijah? And why do you want revenge?"

"Well," he says reluctantly and starts to tremble, "He was my older brother. Someone killed him. I saw it and swore to get even! The Bible says "An eye for an eye." "But the Bible also says "Vengeance belongs to the Lord. Did you report it to the police? When did this happen?"

"I tried that. They ruled it self-defense because they all lied. They said my brother attacked them and they were in fear for their lives." He starts to cry again. "It happened years ago but it still feels like it was yesterday." Then he screams in agony. "I want my family back!"

I hold him close. He buries his head in my chest. We finally go back to bed holding each other tightly.

The next morning, I woke to the smell of freshly brewed coffee, toast, and bacon. Elliot was fixing me breakfast. My arms are sore; my shoulders have purplish bruises. I cover them with foundation and put on a red tee and blue-jean 'daisy dukes'. He was wearing a pair of checkered grey and black boxers and a black *Under Armor* tank top. I run over to him and hug him from behind kissing him gently on his shoulder.

"Sit down beautiful and let me serve you!"

"Thanks, babe! Oh, about last night,"

"Let's not talk about it right now, okay? Let's just eat."

I knew that was my cue to leave it alone. "Okay," I said reluctantly.

He put on some "Boney James" jazz music. "I'm going to get dressed. I have to get to work." He pulls a small black leather bag from behind the couch. He must have brought it in when he came. I don't remember seeing him bringing it in.

"So, what do you do, businessman and where are you from?" I asked jokingly.

"I told you I'm from Kelton. A couple of years ago, I moved to Charlestown about a half hour outside of Sumnerfield. I couldn't bear living at the estate anymore, so I sold it. Now I sell medical equipment to various hospitals across the Midwest region. I'm the top seller!" He proudly boasts.

"That requires a lot of traveling doesn't it?"

"Yes, beautiful, and it brings a lot of money." He yells from the shower.

"Can I come with you sometime?"

"It's too boring for you beautiful and you need my undivided attention. We will have plenty of time together."

He comes out of the shower and kisses me on my neck!

After dressing, he asks, " When will you tell them about your engagement?"

"I was thinking when I go with Grandma to visit Mama. I'm going to meet Sierra for drinks tonight and tell her. She and I go for drinks every other Thursday night at six o'clock."

"Oh, the annoying heifer."

"Baby, please don't call her that. You need to get to know her. She's my best friend."

"Nah she ain't! I'm your bestie now. She got to go!" "Look, that's not going to happen. She's like a sister

to me. She's part of my family." I said angrily.

He grabs me from behind to comfort me. "All I'm saying, Rayna, is that I don't want anyone or anything to come between us. I've never felt this way towards another woman before. I don't want to come second in your life. That's all."

"Baby, you're not going to be second to Sierra but you will come second to God."

"Okay, you got jokes. Did you call your Dad to tell him?"

"Not yet. I will let him know."

"Good. Hey, I've gotta go now, baby. I will call you later. This is my week to be on the road. I won't see you until next Friday but we will talk every day. Save my "cookies"!" He hugged and kissed me and left.

I can't wait to call Sierra and see Grandma and Mama! I'm getting married!!

CHAPTER 16

A SPECIAL VISIT WITH MAMA

"Grandma, what time are we leaving to visit Mama?" "I'll be ready by eleven. We should get there by 11:30

so we can have refreshments with her." "Okay. I will pick you up."

"All right, Ray."

I can't wait to see their reaction to my engagement! Sierra was upset with me when I told her. Of course,

she thinks it's a big mistake. "You're too young and he's a fool!, she said, "We haven't even lived our *best* lives yet, Ray, and you're already talking marriage!"

I assured her that Elliot and I were in love. I told her how he was a top salesman of medical equipment. She didn't care. She suggested I could do better than that.

When I told her about Elliot's nightmare, she wanted me to "dump him quick!"

Geesh! I don't think Sierra and Elliot will ever get along.

Grandma is dressed in a beautiful royal blue and white

pinstripe jumpsuit with matching Sketchers. "You go, Flo! Looking good, Grandma!

"You're all aglow, baby girl! I know that look! You opened that door and your legs, didn't you?" she said laughingly.

"Grandma, c'mon!"

She stares at me and shakes her head.

Mama is waiting for us in the waiting area. We are so excited to see her. Grandma and I give her a big kiss and hug.

Mama holds my hand as she always does. "Mama," I say candidly, "You look amazing!" "Thanks, baby girl!" she says rubbing my hand.

"What's this?"

"Oh, um!"

"Um, what?" Grandma asked. "Well, Elliot proposed to me!"

"Are you sure about this Ray?" Mama sounded extremely concerned. "You're so young, baby girl."

"I know, Mama, but I love him!"

"It's lust I tell you," says Grandma, "You haven't even lived yet, and sitting up here talking about you in love.

You just in heat."

"Look, listen, and learn both of you. I'm a grown woman who can make up her own freaking mind. I'm not asking for your consent or blessing. I would love to have it but I'm marrying him regardless of what either of you say!"

"Whoa, baby girl. We don't mean to upset you, sweetie. We just want what's best for you, Ray. I don't want you to wind up like me and your Daddy."

"Speaking of which," says Grandma, "Have you called him?"

"What do you mean, "called him"?" Mama sounded interested. "You know where your Daddy is?"

"Uh, Carol, I hired a private eye to find him and he did. I hope you're not upset with me."

"No, Mama. I'm good. Where is he? How is he?" Mama sounds excited.

"Mama, I'm not sure where he's staying but he is married."

She doesn't appear to be shocked or saddened by the fact. She looks relieved.

"Did you hear what she said, Carol? You okay?" Grandma asked.

"I'm okay, Mama. I'm glad for him. He deserves someone who can love him unconditionally."

"You do too, Carol."

"I'm afraid the '*Love Boat*' has sailed past me, Mama.

I don't want to board it anymore. I want to get my life back and be here to help my daughter plan a wedding!" She looks at me and smiles.

"Oh, Mama, do you mean it?"

"Of course I do. You my baby girl!"

We hug each other tightly and I start to cry.

"Well, I'm not sold yet," said Grandma, "I need to talk to the young fella."

"Hello everyone!" A male voice replied. We all turn around.

"Pastor Nolan!" Grandma and I say together. "Hi, James. How are you?"

Grandma and I look at Mama who suddenly looks as though the '*Love Boat*' has made a sharp U-turn.

"I'm doing fine, Carol, and hope you are." Pastor Nolan shyly replies.

Mama chuckles like a schoolgirl, "I'm doing good. Do you know these two? This is my Mama, Florence, and my daughter, Rayna."

"Oh yes. I saw you both at Pastor Johnson's anniversary a few months ago."

"Pastor Nolan, what are you doing here? If you don't mind my asking."

"Grandma!"

"It's okay, daughter. Well, Sister Florence, the Word says those who are sick should seek a physician and that's why I'm here. My mind needs medical attention. I'm not ashamed to get help for my mental illness. I suffer from PTSD, anxiety, and depression from the loss of my family. I've been ignoring the symptoms for months, got off my meds, and started self-medicating with painkillers and alcohol. So, I'm here before getting back out there to preach God's word. I can't give to others when I need deliverance myself."

"Oh, James, how touching. This is so brave of you."

Mama sounded impressed and heartfelt.

"Pastor Nolan, did you have a visitor today? Elliot, maybe?"

"Grandma! Please stop being so nosy."

"No, Sister Florence, he's away on business. But my son stopped by!"

"Your son? I thought Elliot announced your son died in a fire." I'm sounding nosy like Grandma.

"James Jr. did, unfortunately," he says with tear-filled eyes, "But my son, Benjamin was by a lady I briefly dated

my Senior year of college. She didn't tell me about him until right before she died of breast cancer. He will be twenty-seven on September 3rd."

"That's my birthday as well," I said excitedly. "Wait, you're Rayna! Elliot did mention that he was

dating you. He seems happy."

"Yes, he has asked me to marry him!" I showed him my ring.

"Lovely ring!" He stares at it with tears in his eyes. "You okay, James?"

"Yeah," he seems distracted now, "I'm happy for Elliot. I hope..." Then he stops talking and says, "I apologize for all my rambling. Carol enjoy your visit with your family and I'll talk with you later, okay?" As he walks away, he hugs me and whispers, "*Pray before you do dear.*"

Chills run down my spine. What does he mean? "Earth to Ray," Grandma waves her hand in front of
my face, "You okay? What did Pastor Nolan say?" "Nothing Grandma."

"Uh, Carol looks like you have an admirer, honey! "Ah, Mama!

"I'm glad! I hope something comes of it. You need a good man in your life."

"Mama, can I get well, please? and I don't need anyone who is just as broken as I am."

"So proud of you Mama!" Grandma and I give her a big hug.

"When are you going to tell your Daddy the good news? Will you let him walk you down the aisle?"

"I was planning on calling him tonight. I think we need to rekindle our relationship first. I mean, he may not even want to."

"Of course, he would. He's your Daddy and you're his baby girl."

"Yeah Ray-Ray, you're Raymond's pride and joy!

Grandma reassured me. "Okay, I will talk to him."

The counselor announces over the intercom, "Families and friends thank you for visiting with us today. We hope to see you here again in October for graduation.

Safe travels."

"Good night, Mama. I'll call you as soon as I talk to Daddy."

"Okay, baby. And congratulations!"

"Love you, Carol. Your Daddy and I are so proud of you!"

"Thanks, Mama. I've never stopped talking to him, you know. Daddy was my biggest hero. I realize now that he's been with me all this time. I miss seeing him, but I know he's with me. Oh, I love you Mama for always believing in me."

"Of course, sweetie. You're my baby girl!"

As we say our goodbyes, I feel eyes watching me. I look around. No one. I feel chills roll down my spine as I remember what Pastor Nolan said, *"Pray before you do, dear."*

What does he mean?

CHAPTER 17

WHO'S BENJAMIN ROBERT MURPHY?

"Hey Mom, what time is he coming?" "Patience, Benji. Around 1:00." "How did you find him?"

"Through a mutual acquaintance that we went to high school with. Marianne's a friend of my Principal, and I think she's also a member of his church."

Adele stumbles to the floor. "Mom, you okay?"

"Yeah, just a little tired that's all." "Here, lie on the couch."

He helped her to the couch in the living room and got her some water.

"When is your next appointment for chemo?" Benjamin asked with worry.

"Next week, baby. You're such a good son. Thank you for looking after me."

"You don't have to thank me, Mom. I'm your son and I love you."

"I know but it's so hard on you. You're so mature for a seventeen-year-old. I wish I had taken better care of myself, baby."

"Getting cancer is not your fault." There's a knock at the door.

"Hi, I'm here to check on you and your Mom."

"Hi, Grandma. She's lying down in the living room. Come on in." "Hi, Mom."

Adele's mother, Shirley, notices how frail she looks. She tries not to seem worried.

Shirley hugs Adele and asks, "When is James coming?" "He said he will be here around 1:00."

"Well, that's in ten minutes," she looks at Benjamin and asks, "Are you okay?"

"Yeah, but a little nervous. I hope he likes me. I wonder if he'll let me meet his wife and my siblings."

"Sweetie, your Mom and I agreed that when the time comes, I will be your legal guardian."

"Oh," sounding disappointed.

"You will still get to know your Dad, baby. It's just that I'm doing what I think is best. I don't want you to be mistreated, okay? You have to understand." Then Adele starts coughing.

"It's okay, Mom. Don't worry. I understand."

He rushes over to give her some water and a hug. There's a knock at the door. Shirley rushes to get it.

She peeps through the peephole. It's James Nolan, Sr.

Shirley opens the door. "Welcome, come on in."

He removes his hat and follows her to the living room.

Immediately it's as though James was beholding his face in a looking glass. There Benjamin stood: bald, pale light skin, muscular, average height, handsome, with hazel eyes.

James ran over and grabbed Benjamin who was stiff as a board. "You look exactly like me and James, Jr." he gasped with excitement.

Shirley and Adele were not surprised at the look- a-likes. They always knew that Benjamin was the spitting image of his father.

"Son," he hugged him again, "Oh, my boy. I apologize but I didn't even know at the time. I'm so sorry son." James looks at Adele and rushes to her side with tear- filled eyes. "I'm so sorry, Adele. What can I do? What do you need?"

"It's a little late for that don't you think?" Benjamin said angrily.

"Son, I."

"Stop calling me 'son'!" My name is *Benjamin*." his voice was trembling.

There was a pause between them as Shirley stepped in. "Benji, please forgive your Grandpa and me for not accepting Adele dating a black man back then. Those were not good times for accepting interracial couples.

Oh, baby, we were fools. Forgive us."

"Yes, and me," Adele said softly, "I didn't even tell your father, I was pregnant. I was afraid he would stay. He was going away to theological school after graduation. I felt it would interrupt." She was in writhing pain and started coughing more this time. She could hardly catch her breath.

"Grandma, can you get her pills and some water, please? They're on the counter in the kitchen."

Shirley got the pills and water while James and Benjamin both sat by her. Neither wanted to leave her side.

James looked at Benjamin remorsefully. Benjamin turned away and looked at his mother.

"You two go into the study to talk; especially now," Adele begged. "Please, Benji. It's important to listen to what your father has to say. For me? Please."

They went into the study. James sat on the sofa while Benjamin sat at the desk staring out the window.

James began to look around the room and noticed Adele's classroom pictures with her fifth-grade students. One plaque read: *"2000 Teacher of the Year Adele Murphy Charlestown Elementary School..."*

"Do you have any idea how hard it was for me growing up without you? Always feeling abandoned or not good enough. Kids teased me often. I resented not having a Dad in my life for so long. Then Mom." Tears streaming down. "Mom is so sick!" He cried.

James ran over and grabbed him, "Son, I'm here now. I'll never leave you again. I'm sorry it happened to you. I didn't know. I'm here. I want to get to know you and then I want you to get to know your family. My family."

"You mean it?"

"Yeah, sure." He hugged him tighter and took out his phone to show him the photos. He smiled when he learned he had twin sisters and a brother. "I can't wait to meet them. Wow! I do look just like him...my younger brother."

Adele was very sick that day. "James, she said, "will you please promise me that you won't abandon him?

That you will check on him from time to time? He will be staying with Mother."

"Yes, I promise, Adele." He began to cry and hugged her.

Adele went back and forth for breast cancer treatment but did not survive. She died that summer in July.

James went to the funeral at Charlestown Missionary Baptist Church and the repast. He kept his word to Adele and Benjamin. He and the kids (without Trudie) went to Benjamin's events in high school, including graduation.

Their bond became inseparable even though Trudie forbade him to see Benjamin. The children never spoke of their secret outings.

CHAPTER 18

DADDY'S POP-UP VISIT

S o good to be home. I think I'll pour myself a glass of wine. I turn on some jazz and start to think of my consummation with Elliot. I wish he were here. I can't wait to tell him about '*Uncle James*' son.

There is a piece of paper on the end table near the lamp in my living room. Daddy's number. I wonder if he's still awake where he is. After all, it is 9:00. Maybe I'll call him in the morning.

I can't sleep so I call Elliot. It's 11:30. No answer. He must be sleeping. I will call him tomorrow.

I turn on the T.V. hoping there's a movie on that will help me go to sleep. "*Sleeping with the Enemy*" is on. I'm a huge Julia Roberts fan. I loved her tenacity in this movie. Well, I will be up for another couple of hours. So much for sleeping.

The movie is over and I begin to drift off to sleep when Elliot calls me. It's 3:00 in the morning.

"Hello, beautiful."

"Hi, Elliot." I purposely sounded tired and yawned.

"How was your visit with your Mom?"

"It was fine. Where were you earlier? I called you." "Did you tell her about your engagement?"

"Yes. She said she can't wait to help plan the wedding."

"Oh, she doesn't have to worry about that and neither do you. Everything will be taken care of. You just have to put on your lovely white gown and be as beautiful as you are. Your family will learn that you are mine now. I will take care of you. They must respect that."

"We'll talk about it when you return. Where were you when I called?"

"Look, are you my Mommy or my fiancée? Don't question me. You're talking to me now, aren't you? Dang, Rayna! I'm tired. I will talk to you tomorrow. I do love you, you know. Have you talked to your Dad yet?"

"I'm calling him this morning around 10:00. Don't be upset. I love you too, baby. I'm sorry, okay?"

"Sure, get some rest, Beautiful. Love you." "Love you too."

When I hang up the phone, I can't help but remember Pastor Nolan's words. I finally go back to sleep.

I awakened to a loud knock at my door! "What in the world? Hold your horses. I'm coming!"

"Ray-Ray!" It's a male's voice.

I look at the time...10:27. "It's not Elliot," I thought. "Who is it?" I yelled as I grabbed a knife from the kitchen.

"It's me, baby girl. We need to talk."

"Daddy!" I'm trippin' I think to myself.

"Please let me in, Ray-Ray."

I run over to the living room window to make sure it's him before I open the door and put the knife away.

"Crap! It is him. Daddy's here!" I slowly open the door. "Daddy?" "Hey, baby girl."

Here he stands well dressed, tall, pecan tan, and handsome. Longer dreads past his shoulders. He looks clean and sober. I can't believe it!

"Come in and have a seat. Do you drink coffee? I'm getting ready to make some." I said while putting the knife back in the drawer.

"Sure, I'll take a cup." He's looking around her luxury apartment. "This is nice, Ray-Ray. You seem to be doing pretty well for yourself."

"Yeah, I do alright. I'm an RN at the hospital in the pediatric unit..."

"Just like your Grandma Florence. I'm not surprised. She did an awesome job with you." He looks saddened by that statement.

"Daddy, you don't have anything to beat yourself up about. I get it. You and Mama made some terrible choices. Life goes on. We grow and we learn from our mistakes. I'm glad you're here. I still love you, Daddy." I hug him and kiss him on the cheek.

"I love you too. How is your Mama, Ray-Ray?"

"She's doing fine now that she's in the Recovery and Rehabilitation Center for Addicts. She graduates from the program in a few months."

"That's awesome, Ray-Ray! You and Florence must be so proud. I'm proud of her. Happy for her." He smiles as if he remembers something from their past.

"Daddy, why didn't you and Mama ever marry?"

"Your Mama didn't want to. I mean, we were young and still in high school. She said I would only be marrying her out of pity and not for love. Your grandparents said we could live with them only if we got married and they would help out with you. They said we couldn't *shack up* in their house. That really upset your Mama. I did love her Ray-Ray. You have to believe that. We both worked hard while we went to school. When I was 18, I found that tiny apartment. I know it wasn't the best but it was all we could afford. Please forgive me baby girl for making so many bad decisions." He cried.

"Daddy, you and Mama don't need to continue asking me for forgiveness, I love you both. All is forgiven.

Grandma and Grandpa explained to me how life was hard on you both. It's like you couldn't catch a break and drugs is where you found a way of escape. I'm so grateful that you both have found a new avenue of peace. I pray you stay on the straight and narrow path."

I didn't realize I was crying until I felt the taste of my salty tears. Daddy got us both some Kleenex. We drank another cup of coffee and talked about the model cars he taught me to build.

"Look at the time! I'm going to walk around the park for a few minutes. You wanna come?" He asked.

"Well, I have to get some sleep before going to work. How long are you going to be here? I'm off Thursday and Friday."

"Perfect! I'm here until Thursday, I leave Friday at 7 a.m."

"That's too bad because I was hoping you could meet my fiancée!" I said showing him my ring.

"What? So who's the lucky guy."

"His name is Elliot Nolan."

Daddy looked as though he had seen a ghost. "What's the matter, Daddy?"

"N-N-Nothing Ray-Ray. Where is he from?"

"Kelton."

"Oh, Lord!" Daddy seemed frightened.

"Daddy, what's wrong? You're making me nervous."

"Oh, Ray-Ray. Remember, when I left Sumnerfield because I told you I wanted to get clean and I couldn't do it here? Well, I went to Kelton. A fancy town of lawyers, doctors, and judges? Bout three hours from here."

"Yeah, I know where it is."

"I took a bus there. I heard they had a great rehab and recovery center there, so I wanted to check in. Well, a friend and I felt I should shoot up one more time before getting straight and unfortunately, I did. I hit a car because it was raining so hard that night. It was a terrible storm. We could hardly see or tell what was in front of us. I was so high, Ray. When I woke up in the driver's seat, I had killed a lawyer and a well-known singer. That night was such a blur." He started crying inconsolably.

"Daddy, did they have children?"

"Yeah, two boys. I think. Maybe, one son. I can't remember it was about seventeen years ago. What a tragic night it was. I was arrested and sent to Firth County State Prison for 10 years. That's where I met Tasha. She was a nurse in the infirmary. She was good to me. We married not long after I finished doing my time and now we have twins. My son's name...I mean your brother's name is Anthony Ray and your little sister's name is Latisha Rae. They're getting ready to turn 7 years old on December 18."

"Well, don't forget my birthday is coming up next month on September 3rd." I sounded like some spoiled brat.

"I can't forget my firstborn, Ray-Ray! I couldn't send anything because I was in prison and too ashamed by the time I got out. I thought you hated me for leaving you. I was afraid to reach out."

"Oh, Daddy!" I give him a big hug. "When can I meet them and Tasha?"

"Well, I need to talk it over with her first, okay? I thought you would be angry once you found out."

He shows me pictures of his wholesome family. The little boy must look like Tasha and the little girl is the spitting image of me. I can't help but smile and shed tears of joy. I have a little sister and brother!

"Are you kidding? I hated being the only child."

Then I see tears rolling down Daddy's face and I give him some Kleenex.

"Is Elliot their son, Ray-Ray?"

"Yes, Daddy. He is," I say reluctantly.

"I'm sorry, baby girl."

"It's okay, I will talk to him. Everything will work out. You'll see."

"I don't think I can go to the wedding, sweetie. I don't think it would be healthy for me. I think I'll go back to Kelton in the morning. I'm sorry."

"Daddy, I understand. But we haven't set a date yet. Who knows the wedding could be next year on my twenty-fourth birthday. A lot could change between now and then."

He finally left after our hugs and goodbyes and we planned to see each other again...next time in Kelton.

Chapter 19

ONE BIG FIGHT

It's Friday, but I'm certainly not feeling excited. Elliot's coming over and I have to tell him about Daddy.

Wait! I need to talk to the noisy, nosy bunch: Mama, Grandma, and Sierra.

Crap! Elliot's calling me. I can't answer it. He's going to be upset. It's still ringing.

"Hey, babe."

"Why you ain't picking up the phone?"

"Elliot, we need to talk when you get here."

"What is it now, Rayna?" he says angrily.

"I'd rather tell you in person."

"Oh, here we go again. I guess you don't want to get married now, huh?"

"Look, we will talk when you get here!" I hung up the phone.

He calls back but I don't answer. I need to talk to Sierra.

"C'mon, Sierra, pick up your phone."

"What's up, girl?

"It's not good? Elliot's parents were killed by my Daddy."

"What? Ray, are you sure? How do you know that?"

"Because Daddy popped up for a visit and told me. He's also married and has twins...a boy, Anthony, and a girl, Latisha. They're six years old."

"Wait! You have siblings! Oh my goodness, I'm coming over!"

"No! Elliot is coming over, Sierra, and I have to tell him."

"Are you crazy, Ray-Ray? You don't need to tell him without someone being there. He could snap!"

"I don't believe he will. I can't keep this from him especially if we're talking about getting married."

"Girl, if this ain't proof that you shouldn't marry him then I don't know what is. Let me come over...*please*."

"No. I will call you later. Listen, I believe that's him at the door now." I hung up before Sierra could finish her sentence. I'm contemplating now as to whether Elliot and I should be married. "Lord, help me." I think to myself as I answer the door.

"Woman, you better not ever hang a phone up on me again."

Elliot is furious. His fists are tightly clenched again.

"Listen, Elliot, I don't know if I can marry you because my Daddy is the one who hit your parents."

He stares at me. His eyes are fierce-looking.

Crying...tears pouring down his face. He falls to the floor in disbelief. His mind goes back to that day when he and Elijah had to go live with their uncle and aunt.

The rage he felt on the inside. He looks wildly around the room. He doesn't seem human anymore.

Suddenly, he upends my couch, flips over the coffee table, breaks several dishes, and punches a hole in the kitchen wall. His knuckles are bleeding. He doesn't care. He comes after me. Hysterical. He looks barbaric.

Almost demonic.

Something is telling me to "Run!" but my feet are paralyzed by fear. I can't move. He wraps his hand around my throat. I can't breathe. I start clawing at his face. I finally break free while kicking him where the sun doesn't shine. He fell to the floor. I ran to my room and locked myself in.

"Elliot, please leave before I call the police. The marriage is off. Please go!"

"You won't hear from me again, Rayna. I promise."

When he left, I wept inconsolably for hours.

Sierra called me, but I didn't answer. Grandma called, and I still didn't answer.

I don't want to talk to anyone. I want to be alone.

After a couple of days, I heard loud knocking at the door. I look out my window and here's two from the *noisy, nosy bunch* like a church caravan. Mama's not with them for obvious reasons.

"Open this door, Ray-Ray! yelled Grandma.

"Or we will bust it open." echoes Sierra.

"I'm coming!" I holler back. I finally opened the door.

"My goodness, you look a mess. What's that on your neck? Is that a bruise?"

"I'm okay, Grandma."

Sierra starts crying. I've never seen her like this.

"Don't cry, Sierra," I hug her. "I'm okay. I called off the wedding."

"Praise Jesus!" shouted Grandma.

"For what it's worth, I am sorry Ray-Ray," Sierra's still wiping away her tears, "but you deserve better than *a piece of a man*. I'm glad you see what he's like now before you said 'I do'."

"I know, Sierra, but I love him!" I started crying.

"Nonsense, chile, ain't no way you can love or want to be with someone that's beating on you. I don't care how fine he is or how much money he got."

"Grandma, he just found out that Daddy is responsible for his parent's death, and he lost it. That's all!"

"What? Your Daddy did what?" Grandma seems shaken now.

"That's right! Daddy said he went to prison for ten years because of it. He said it was raining hard that night and he couldn't see. He decided he wanted to get high one more time before admitting himself to rehab. He hit this well-known couple. The woman was a lawyer and the man was a famous gospel singer. They were Elliot's parents. Elliot was just a kid when it happened. So now you understand why he flipped out. Right?"

"Ray-Ray is he getting therapy?" Sierra appeared very concerned now.

"I don't think so."

"I still say he should not have attacked you, Ray."

"Grandma, it was a mistake! He didn't mean it!"

"Ah please, Ray-Ray, abusers never *__mean it__* and you know it. That's how abusers are. They do it, promise to never do it again, bear you with gifts, have make-up sex, and the cycle continues. Stay away from him, please. He needs serious professional help, and you can't give it to him."

"Grandma, I understand what you're saying but Elliot loves me. It won't happen again."

"Oh stop, Ray-Ray," Sierra yelled angrily, "You don't think I saw those bruises on your shoulders a few weeks ago? I should have said something but I didn't. I know you were trying to hide it with foundation. And you say *__I'm__* not supportive."

"What bruises, Ray-Ray?" Grandma is mad and frustrated with me now.

"It's okay guys, he was having a nightmare about his brother, Elijah. He saw him get killed by someone and, he accidentally shook me."

"I tell you, Ray, he's psychotic. You can't go back to him." Sierra warned.

"I love him," I screamed at them, "Don't you understand? Get out! Both of you! Get out!"

I open the door. They're staring at me. Neither of them are moving. Just standing there looking at me as though I'm crazy. Out of my mind.

Calmly Sierra says, "Ray, sweetie, you need to come with me. You've just suffered a traumatic experience. Look around you. He ransacked your house and, you look a hot mess. Take a look in the mirror."

"Listen to her baby." Grandma is crying now.

"I respect what you are saying, but I'm fine. Please go. I wanna be alone now. I need to clean up, take a shower, and relax. Luckily, I don't have to work tonight."

"Okay, baby. Will you please call me tomorrow?"

"Sure, Grandma." I kiss her on the cheek and she squeezes me tightly.

"If you don't call me tomorrow, Ray-Ray, I'm coming over here and bust your door down," shouted Sierra on her way out. I give Sierra a hug.

"I promise guys. I will call you. I just need to think."

I look around the room after they finally leave. I assess the damage. Probably around $5,000 bucks. I'll have to make some calls tomorrow.

I ran into my room and shut the door. I cried for hours.

"Pray before you do, dear." Pastor Nolan's voice rang in my ears with those words as I fell asleep.

CHAPTER 20

TASHA'S DISQUIETUDE

"I'm glad you're home baby." Tasha leaps up and gives Raymond a big kiss and hug, right in front of the children. "Ugh!" they both shout with laughter.

He grabs them and kisses them while giving them a big bear hug.

Tasha notices he seems depressed and disheartened. "Kids go play in the den. Daddy and I need to talk. Okay?"

"Okay, Mommy. Welcome home, Daddy."

"Thanks. Love you, kids." They run off to play, teasing each other.

"You okay, baby? How was your visit?"

"Not good, honey. I mean, Ray-Ray is doing great."

"Ray-Ray? That's her name?"

"It's Rayna. We call her 'Ray-Ray.'"

"Oh, okay. Come sit down baby, and tell me all about it."

He wanders to the couch, sits down, and puts his feet on the ottoman.

"Well, apparently, I killed her fiancée's parents on that rainy night when I was high."

"What? Baby, no!" Tasha gasped.

"Yep. We were catching up and I told her about what happened when I came to Kelton. Then she told me about her fiancée. That's how I found out about his parents. They were his parents, Tasha! I can't even walk 'baby girl' down the aisle because I can't face him. Not after what I've done."

He stands up and starts pacing. He's nervous and rubbing his head. Very agitated.

"Come sit down, baby, please." Massaging his back, Tasha asked, "Did you take your medicine, baby? "

Raymond runs out of the house. Tasha follows him. "Baby, come back inside, please honey. C'mon, you need to take your medicine."

Instead, he falls to the ground screaming at the top of his lungs.

The neighbors start to come outside to see what's going on. They're whispering. The neighbor to the left of them, Mr. Schneider asks whether he should call the police.

"No, he's okay. I need to give him his medicine. He will be fine."

Raymond hears Mr. Schneider's voice. He calms down. He sees the neighbors staring at him with confused looks of concern on their faces.

"C'mon, baby. Let's go inside." Tasha says quietly and nervously.

He stands up and wobbles into the house holding onto Tasha's shoulder.

The kids are still playing. They have no idea what's going on. Laughter is coming from the den.

Tasha gives Raymond his medicine. He lies down and places his head on her lap as they sit on the couch.

"I'm sorry I embarrassed you baby."

"Don't ever apologize to me for that Raymond. You're okay. We will go see Dr. Fitzgerald tomorrow. I will set up an appointment. I'm afraid this news may have caused a setback for you. I don't think seeing your daughter right now is safe or healthy for you."

"I agree. I can't stand thinking about that night, Tasha."

"Did you have a chance to speak to her mother? "No, I left the next morning as soon as Ray-Ray told me about him; her fiancée. His name is Elliot Nolan."

Tasha's eyes squinted as though she remembered something. "Elliot Nolan? I've heard the name before. A few years ago," she remembered.

"Probably about the car accident. I mean, those were his parents, honey." Raymond reminded her.

"No. That's not it. I think this involved another family member's death. A Pastor Nolan's wife."

She kept thinking. Then she grabbed her phone and googled *The Nolans in Kelton.*" An article popped up: *"Trudie Nolan, Pastor's Wife Drowns in Family Pool."* It read:

"On Wednesday, September 3, Trudie Nolan, 47, of House of Prayer Missionary Baptist Church in Kelton, NC, drowned in the family's pool. Mrs. Nolan, a swimming instructor, had alcohol in her system at the time of the drowning. Her death was ruled an accidental drowning due to alcohol poisoning. She is survived by her husband, Pastor James Nolan Sr., James Nolan, Jr. (son), Kayla, and Kristen Nolan(daughters)."

"See baby," showing him her phone, "I remember reading this article and thinking about her children. There was also another incident about a year later... *September 3rd*. It was about a house fire but the Pastor's alibi checked out so he wasn't charged. His children died. His entire family. Gone. That poor man."

Raymond sits up, squeezes his head, and rocks back and forth wanting to forget the tragedy, "I don't want to remember anymore. The pain..."

"Baby, it's okay to remember. It was real. What you did was real and you can't blot it out as though it never happened. You have to face it, baby. That's the only way you will get better. We will see Dr. Fitzgerald tomorrow."

"Okay, I just wanna get some rest now."

The twins ran into the living room. "Mommy, we're hungry!"

Raymond goes into the bedroom to take a nap while Tasha makes lunch for the kids. She's apprehensive about Raymond's well-being now.

"I don't think Raymond's daughter or her mother should be in his circle. I will have to see what Dr. Fitzgerald says tomorrow." Tasha says to herself.

CHAPTER 21

PASTOR NOLAN SHARES A MEMORY

"Good morning, Carol. It's a lovely day."

"It sure is, James. Did you sleep well last night?"

"No, not really. I tossed and turned. Restless about my family. I miss them so much, Carol. They meant the world to me."

"I can only imagine. Losing your entire family, I mean. I'm so sorry for your loss. Such devastation."

She places her hand over his. It's warm. She smiles at him.

"Do you mind if I sit with you?" he asks with tears in his eyes.

"Sure. I could use the company." She blushes.

"You're easy to talk to Carol. It's like...you listen without judgment. You know what I mean?"

"Yeah, I get that a lot. Easy listener. So go ahead. Talk." She feels disappointed.

"Such a beautiful soul!" he whispers.

"What?"

"Oh, nothing," he says shyly.

"Sadly, I lost Trudie long before she died," he continues the conversation, "She was upset with me when I told her about my son, Benjamin. I told her it was a fling I had during college, and it was before I met her. She wouldn't believe me or forgive me. We argued on the day she died because she did not want me to go see him. It was his 18th birthday and I promised his Mom on her deathbed that I would be there for him. I couldn't break that promise."

As he cried, Carol gave him some Kleenex.

"Over the years, I became ill and started drinking to fill the void. I didn't pay attention to the Word of God or my children. I was filled with grief and anger. I don't understand how she drowned though. She was a swimming instructor. They said she had been drinking before she died, but Trudie wasn't a drinker. She hated the smell of booze." He hit the table with his fists.

Carol flinched. She touched his arm and said softly, "It's okay, James."

He looked into her beautiful, soft brown eyes and a calm came over him. "Carol, I'm sorry if I made you nervous. Thank you for listening."

"I'm okay. I understand your frustration. I'm glad you are here getting the help you need to cope with all of it. C'mon, let's go for a walk."

On the walking trail, they start to learn more about each other. James wants to know about her drug dependency. Carol seems resistant talking about it but realizes that she enjoys conversing with him.

"I didn't ask to get addicted. No one does," Carol said as they stopped to sit on a bench, "but getting high started as fun. Something to pass the time. Raymond, Ray-Ray's Dad, and I were just high school kids experimenting with recreational drugs...weed mostly and coke a few times. One of Raymond's buddies asked us to try heroin when we worked at the pharmaceutical company. The rest is histo ry...that's what brought me here."

"No, I think *this* led us to each other," James said, "I don't believe it's by chance but by faith that we arrived here at the same time. We could be a testimony for many brothers and sisters in Kelton."

"One sobriety day at a time. That's what we strive for, James. Only God can fix the brokenness and brokenhearted. We can't fix each other or save others

until we have overcome our obstacles...faced our demons. No offense, but if the Pastor falls off the bandwagon what becomes of the flock."

"Spoken like a true woman of God, *me lady*," he bows and gently kisses her hand.

While giving him a bashful yet flirtatious grin she pulls her hand away.

"It's time for my therapy session and I don't want to miss it," she begins to walk away. Suddenly, she turns around to him and says, "If you don't mind, I would rather concentrate on my sobriety and getting well. You understand, right?"

"Sure, Carol. I understand. We both need deliverance and healing. If it is the Lord's will, we will talk **after** the program."

"Perhaps, but no promises, kind sir."

"One day at a time, right? he says disappointed.

"One sobriety day at a time, Pastor."

Carol walks away smiling. She glances back and he is still watching her with a smile from Earth to Heaven.

CHAPTER 22

SECOND THOUGHTS

I don't believe it! Not one phone call from Elliot. My heart is aching as it did when Granddaddy died. I want to call him to see how he's doing.

My phone rings. Is it Elliot?

"Good morning, Ms. Jennings. This is Bobby from BB's Fix-it and Repairs. I was calling to let you know we are running a little behind with our first project this morning and won't get to you until after lunch around 1:00. Is this okay with you?"

"Sure, that's fine," Rayna says morosely.

She looks around the living room and the kitchen. Still in shock and disbelief that it all happened. What a mess! The living room and kitchen looked like it was hit by a tornado.

"Why hasn't he called?" she whispered to herself.

She carefully shuffles through the debris into the kitchen to make coffee.

The phone rings. "Elliot?" she yells.

"No, Ray-Ray, it's me."

"Oh, hey Sierra." I sighed and rolled my eyes.

"I know you're not sitting over there waiting for him to call. You haven't called him have you?"

"No, Sierra! Did you call to check on me or to badger me?" I began to cry.

"Ray-Ray, calm down. Can I come over, please? Just to sit with you. I won't say a word. I promise."

"No, the people are coming over to work on the place. It's going to cost about $4,500."

"For real? $4,500? You better sue him, girl."

"Leave me alone about it, Sierra. Listen, someone's beeping in."

"Someone's beeping in? Is it that fool? Don't answer it!"

"It's Grandma, Sierra. I'll call you back."

"I love you, Ray-Ray. You know that, right?"

"I know sis. Thank you."

I grab some Kleenex to wipe my eyes and sniffle before clicking over to Grandma.

"Hey, Grandma," I try to sound cheerful.

"Hey, baby girl. Can I come over?"

"I do miss you, Grandma. Sure, c'mon."

I fix two cups of coffee and tidy up my den before she comes since the other parts of the house are a mess.

There's a knock at the door and then it opens.

"I'm in the den, Grandma. I fixed us some coffee."

No answer.

"Grandma?" I repeated.

No answer.

I come out from the den. My cup of coffee falls to the marble floor. Shattered glass breaking loudly. In my mind, it sounded like an explosion.

"Elliot, what are you doing here? How did you get in? I..."

"The door must've been unlocked," he said quickly.

No, it wasn't?"

"Okay, I picked the lock. I had to see you, baby. I was afraid if I called that you wouldn't answer. I wanna pay for the damages Rayna. I'm so sorry, baby. I love you so much!"

"You just broke into my home!" The door slowly opens.

"What are you doing here, hoodlum? I'm calling the cops Ray-Ray!"

"Grandma, please don't. He's leaving. He just came by to see if he could pay for the damages."

"Oh, he's gonna pay. And I mean now. Don't give her a check or money order either. Cash only!"

"I got it, Mrs. Jennings." He said sternly with a tight face.

He reaches into his gym bag and pulls out a small gift box and a tan envelope filled with cash. Five thousand dollars cash...*exactly*.

"Elliot, how did you know the estimate?"

He hugged Rayna and gently kissed her on the cheek.

"Goodbye, Rayna! He slowly backed away from her with tear-filled eyes nearly bumping into her grandmother.

"But baby...I mean, Elliot, how did you know the damages were about $5,000."

He turned and ran out the door.

I ran after him. "Elliot, wait!"

He jumped into his car and sped away. Grandma brought me back inside saying, "Ray- Ray good riddance to him. You got the money and he's gone. Maybe now you can start to pick up the pieces and put your life back together."

"Grandma, it still doesn't explain how he knew to give me that amount. The only person who knew was Sierra. I'm going to call her!"

"Sierra, did you see Elliot and tell him how much it was to get my place fixed?"

"Well, *hello* to you too, Ray, and **no**, I didn't.   What's going on?"

"He came over and brought me five thousand dollars. In cash!"

"I'm coming over," She hung up.

Grandma was cleaning up the shattered glass from the coffee cup in the hallway while I put on some more coffee.

Sierra finally arrived. I went to take a shower because the repairmen would arrive shortly.

"Hey, Grandma Flo," yelled Sierra from the kitchen while switching off the coffee pot, "Where y'all at?"

"We're in the den, sweetie. Ray-Ray is taking a shower . She says the repairmen will be here around one o'clock."

Sierra was perplexed. "Just look at this mess. What happened down here?" Sierra sees the broken glass in the dustpan in the hallway.

"**Elliot** happened; that's what. You know that thang had the nerve to pick her lock."

"That's it! I'm calling the cops."

"No, you better not," I warned Sierra as I was getting dressed, "no harm, no foul. Let me handle Elliot."

"I think you're in danger, Ray-Ray. This guy is disturbed."

"Sierra, how many times do I have to tell you he's just hysterical and upset about finding out who killed his parents in the crash? I love him guys and he..."

"What's in this box?" Sierra butted in with her nosy self. "He gave you this, Ray?"

While arguing with them, I had completely forgotten about the small gift box.

"Yes, he did!" I snatched it from her.

Should I open it in front of them? I thought to myself, These noisy, nosey heifers.

"Well, open it!" shouted Grandma.

I carefully opened the small red gift box with a black bow around it. The colors were a reminder of our first date night. I turned my back away from them and felt joy as I opened the box.

"Oh my goodness!" I screamed.

"What is it?" Grandma yelled.

I turned toward them with a smile from Earth to Heaven. He gave me a 1/2 ct. ruby red diamond ring with matching earrings! The card read:

"You are my Queen forever. My Diamond in the ruff. I love you, Rayna."

With teary eyes, Grandma said, "Ain't that much forgiveness in the world. It's not worth your life Ray-Ray. That boy needs help."

Sierra chimed in, "I hope you're not having second thoughts about taking him back and marrying him."

"Will you two please butt out? I know what I'm doing. I will convince Elliot to go to counseling with me."

"Whatever you say, Ray-Ray," Sierra said, her voice conveying a warning.

"C'mon, guys. Will you stop judging me and him and just pray for us?"

"Trust me, you're going to need all the prayer you can get for this one," retorted Grandma with seriousness filling her voice.

The repairmen finally arrived. We decided to eat out and then go to the park while Bobby and his crew worked feverishly to fix the kitchen and living room.

By the time I got home that evening, the crew was finishing up. Grandma and Sierra wanted to come in to check things out before going home.

Standing so proudly with his chest out, Bobby asked, "So, Ms. Jennings, what do you think?

"Oh, this looks awesome guys!"

"Oh my goodness!" chorused Grandma and Sierra in agreement.

I couldn't thank them enough and paid them the entire $5,000. He gave me a few business cards to share with others before he left.

I said my goodbyes to Grandma and Sierra and went to take a shower.

"I'm going to call Elliot tomorrow," I think to myself.

CHAPTER 23

RAYMOND'S TOUGH DECISION

Raymond and Tasha dropped the twins off at Tasha's parents' house before heading to Dr. Fitzgerald's office.

"Let's take the kids to the park afterward, honey. Is that okay with you?" Tasha suggested.

"Sure, baby. That's a great idea."

When Dr. Fitzgerald saw them entering, he welcomed them eagerly and gestured for them to take a seat. Tasha quickly noticed a significant change in his appearance since their last meeting, remarking to herself that he had put on a bit of weight and no longer wore glasses. She couldn't help but think that he looked charming and rather handsome.

"Despite the circumstances, I am delighted to see you two. Can you tell me more about the nature of your visit today?"

"It's good to see you as well, Dr. Fitzgerald," Tasha stated with a warm smile.

Raymond sat in a corner trembling and balling his eyes out.

Speaking loudly over his cries, Dr. Fitzgerald asks Tasha, "What triggered this episode?"

"His daughter and her mother. He went for a visit a couple of days ago and learned that his daughter's fiancée is the son of the parents Raymond hit and killed in a car crash."

"Okay, this is serious." Dr. Fitzgerald documents the information, looks down at his notes, and says, "Mrs. Brown, I think it's best to see him three times a week instead of once."

"Thank you, Doctor. He's been like this since he returned. He's not sleeping either," Tasha says worriedly.

Raymond stopped crying, returned to his seat, and whispered in Tasha's ear.

Dr. Fitzgerald seemed concerned. "Is everything all right?"

"Oh, he's just going to the bathroom. I'm going to step out for some air."

" You don't have to go," Dr. Fitzgerald said.

"Yes, I do. I will return with my husband. Tasha snapped at him.

"I'm sorry for upsetting you, Mrs. Brown. I get it."

"Good." She walked out.

Raymond is still in the bathroom after five minutes and Tasha is frantically waiting in the hallway. "What is taking him so long?" she quietly says.

Dr. Fitzgerald comes into the hallway seeming to be impatient because of Raymond's long bathroom break. "Is Raymond, okay, Mrs. Brown? I have another client in thirty minutes."

"I'm not sure. It shouldn't take this long. Can you check on him, please?"

Dr. Fitzgerald walks into the men's bathroom and quickly yells out, "Call 9-1-1...quick!"

"What happened?" she burst into the bathroom, "Oh my God! Raymond...Raymond, baby!" She's crying hysterically.

Blood everywhere! His wrists were cut!

Dr. Fitzgerald had several paper towels wrapped around Raymond's bloody wrists trying to stop the bleeding. "Mrs. Brown, please call 9-1-1! NOW!" He yells at her.

She quickly grabs her phone from her purse, dials 9-1-1, and starts screaming into the phone. "Please come quick! My husband just slit his wrists. We're at Dr. Fitzgerald's office at the corner of Horne and East Main Street."

"Address is 121 E. Main Street," Dr. Fitzgerald yells out.

"Someone is on the way," the dispatcher speaks calmly.

"Where did he even get something to cut his wrists?" Tasha cries.

Dr. Fitzgerald looks around and discovers a pair of scissors near Raymond's body. He doesn't touch them but points them out to Tasha.

"I don't understand," Tasha is visibly frightened, "He hasn't done anything like this since...since."

"You mean he has tried suicide before, Mrs. Brown?" The police and paramedics arrive. They quickly go to work.

"Well, yes, about a week after coming to Firth County State Prison."

Officers Keegan and Hayworth of the Kelton PD question Tasha and Dr. Fitzgerald. They take their statements and let them know they will be in touch before finalizing their report.

The paramedics transported Raymond to the psychiatric unit of Kelton Memorial Hospital. Tasha rode with Raymond and Dr. Fitzgerald followed suit in a red Lamborghini.

When they arrived at the hospital, Raymond was unconscious from losing so much blood. Tasha phones her parents to explain what happened to Raymond and asks if they could keep the kids until he's released. They agreed and extended their prayers and apologies.

The doctors rushed him to the operating room. Hours passed by as he underwent the surgery. The long and painful hours of recovery seemed never-ending. It was as if time stood still. Finally, as the clock strikes 10 pm, he slowly awakened from the anesthesia.

"Carol! Where's Carol?" Raymond moaned; not fully awake yet.

"What? Carol?" Tasha was angry and began to cry. Raymond finally opened his eyes and said sleepily,

"Don't cry Tasha, please. I'm so sorry. I was just feeling so overwhelmed. I didn't mean to slit my wrists. Baby, I'm going to call Ray-Ray and tell her that I can't give her away. I can't face her fiancee. I don't think it's a good idea for me to go to Sumnerfield anymore."

Tasha tried to remain calm although she was still upset that he said another woman's name...must've been his daughter's Mama. She turned and looked at Raymond but no words would come; only tears.

"Baby, I said I'm sorry. I'm not going to Sumnerfield anymore. Please forgive me. Do you think I'm making the right decision?"

Tasha realized that Raymond probably didn't remember saying the woman's name because he was groggy and drugged up from the anesthesia. She decided to dismiss it for now. She grabbed some Kleenex and wiped her face. She leaned over to hug and kiss him gently on his cheek.

"So do you think I'm doing the right thing, babe? Staying away from Ray-Ray until I get better?"

"I agree with you but let's talk to Dr. Fitzgerald first to be certain this is the right decision. He wants them to keep you in the psychiatric unit for 30 days for observation. He will be in and out checking up on you to make sure that you're safe and receiving the proper care."

Raymond didn't seem shocked at the news of having to stay. "Okay, honey. I love you, Tasha."

After he falls asleep. Dr. Fitzgerald enters the room and puts his arm around Tasha's shoulders to comfort her. She pushes his hand away and backs up.

"Please don't do that. It makes me feel uncomfortable. I'd like to speak to you in the hallway." Tasha said harshly.

He walks with her, his smile seemingly forced. "Listen here, Dr. Fitzgerald, I'm not sure what your game is, but I'm happily and wholeheartedly devoted to my husband. I suggest you keep your focus on your job or we'll have no issue finding someone more suitable for our needs."

"Well, for someone who's 'happily married,' why is your husband calling out for 'Carol' instead of his fine wife?"

Tasha seethed with fury. "Screw it. I'll begin the search for a new doctor first thing in the morning and report you too."

"No, no, no, Mrs. Brown. I'm sorry. It was harmless. I didn't mean to upset you. I will be strictly professional from now on. Please give me another chance."

"Okay," she said hesitantly, "You can start by figuring out what to tell Raymond about his decision not to see his daughter anymore if she marries her fiancée. I don't feel it's a good idea for him to see her or anyone in Sumnerfield right now. He needs to let go of his past."

CHAPTER 24

DISTURBING NEWS ABOUT GRANDPA HARRY

Grandma called. She didn't sound like herself. She'd been crying.

"Grandma, what's wrong?"

"I need to talk to you, Ray-Ray. Can you come over?"

"Sure! I'm on the way."

I slip on some shorts and a tank top and high tail it over there.

When I arrived, she was sitting on the patio around the back. Tissue box and two cups of coffee.

I rush over to hug her. "Grandma, what happened?"

"Please don't marry him, baby. He needs help. He's damaged, Ray."

"Of course, he needs help, Grandma. I am going to talk to him about going to marital counseling."

"No, Ray-Ray," she said crossly, "I mean professional psychiatric help."

"Grandma, he's not crazy; just brokenhearted."

"Ray, I've been where you are with your Granddaddy."

Rayna gasped, "I don't believe you, Grandma! How can you say that? Grandpa never hit you! Did he?"

"Yes, when Carol was around three years old. He was an alcoholic."

"Grandma, I've never seen Grandpa drink a day in my life."

"I know, he went to counseling and a treatment center in Maryland for a year after it happened. He never drank again or hit me again. Elliot needs professional help, baby. Please don't marry him. Not yet."

"I understand, Grandma. But what happened between you and Grandpa? Why did he...you know?" I couldn't bring myself to say it.

"Hit me? Just because you don't say it Ray doesn't mean it didn't happen or that it will go away. The scar will always be with me to remind me. I had to heal on the inside to forgive him from my heart; not just with my mouth. We spent years in therapy and on medication. God pulled us through."

Grandma Flo pulled down her top and showed me the mid-sized scar on her right shoulder. I started crying.

Then I got mad at Grandpa. I looked toward Heaven and shouted, "Grandpa how could you!"

"It's okay, Ray.-Ray It was years ago. He made it right. He gave his life to God and got the proper help. We never had issues like that again."

"Did Mama see him hit you?"

"Yes, I'm afraid so. She was three or four at the time. We spent years trying to make it up to her. To raise her in a nurturing, safe, loving home."

"Oh, man! The things you learn about a person you look up to so much. He was my hero, Grandma."

"He still is, baby. We all have done and said things we are not proud of. We're not perfect people, Ray. No one is. The point is when you know or find out you're sick, you seek God and a physician to be healed; to get well. Without Christ to lead and guide you, you're bound to repeat. That's what's wrong with Elliot. He's out of control."

I reminded Grandma that she still hadn't told me what happened.

Grandma took a deep breath. You can tell the discussion was hard for her. As if she was reliving the past again. With tear-filled eyes, she started talking.

"Well, it was a blizzard that night. I remember because the heat went out and I bundled Carol up under three blankets and a pile of clothes to keep her warm. Harry had been drinking all day. He never drank so much. Something was bothering him. He seemed so agitated. I remained quiet most of the time because I didn't want to rile him. Anyway, I was getting ready for bed and he wanted to make love and I didn't. I couldn't take the smell of that stinkin' alcohol. I told him I didn't want to. But he didn't care. He slapped me and threw me on the bed. We wrestled and he picked up a beer bottle and hit me across my back. I started bleeding because the glass gashed my skin. We heard screaming and looked up. Carol was standing at the door yelling for Harry to stop. He staggered to pick her up but she ran and hid under her bed. I ran past him to get her. He was crying and told me he had lost his job and didn't know how to tell me. He kept apologizing and the next day he called a friend of his who recommended the facility in Maryland. He was gone for a year. He started going to church with me and Carol and received Christ into his life. It was a major turning point for us."

I took some Kleenex and wiped her tears.

"I'm so sorry, Grandma. Now I know why you reacted the way you did. I had no idea. I will give Elliot an ultimatum.

..choose a life with me by getting help for his mental illness or let me go."

"That's not the way it works, Ray-Ray. He has to want the help and accept that he has a problem."

"I hear you, Grandma. Love you. Love you. Love you."

CHAPTER 25

RAYNA'S ULTIMATUM

I thought about what Grandma and I discussed concerning abuse and mental illness. It is not that I am ignoring our discussion but I don't want to lose Elliot.

I'll give him an ultimatum. I'm going to call him when I get home.

After I took a shower, I realize I have a couple of hours before I have to lie down for work. I slip on my 'Betty Boop' pajama set and call Elliot.

No answer. My heart sinks in my chest. I wait 15 minutes and try again. Still no answer.

I go into my newly renovated kitchen to pour myself a glass of wine when the doorbell rings. I pray it's Elliot. I ran to the door to open it.

"Hi, can I help you?"

The chocolate, handsome, well-dressed man looks me up and down as if he approves of my figure and says, "I sure hope so, Miss. I was told to give you this." He hands me a red gift box and envelope.

"And your name is?"

"Not important. Good night, Ma'am." He tipped his hat and walked away with a smile on his face.

I shook my head and tossed the gift and envelope on the couch. I called Elliot again.

Still no answer. "Where could he be? And who was that man?" I thought.

I drifted off to sleep before it was time to go to work.

About a couple of hours later, the doorbell rang. I jumped up and ran to the door.

"Who is it?" I yelled, feeling frustrated.

"Can we talk, baby?"

"Elliot!" I flung the door open and he came on in, grabbed me, and began kissing me all over. I welcomed every second; every minute of his touch.

"Oh, how I missed you, Rayna!" he said.

"I missed you too but, I have to go to work."

"Not tonight, I need you!" He whisked me away in his arms and carried me to the bedroom where we made love a few times.

I called out of work. I lied to my supervisor that I wasn't feeling well. They knew about the issues I had been having so she quickly excused me and told me to get better soon.

Elliot was in the shower and I went to join him. We made love again.

"I can't live without you, Rayna. I don't want to. I'd rather kill myself than live without you."

"Don't say that, Elliot! Don't ever say that again!"

"But it's true! If I can't have you, I don't wanna live! It's too painful without you."

We both began to cry and held each other tightly.

I said, "There's one condition, Elliot. We have to go to counseling and you have to get professional help for your anger issues."

He sat up. His face was tight. "You trying to give me an ultimatum, Rayna?"

"If you care about us and want us to get married, then yes. I guess I am."

My eyes fill with tears. I expect him to say 'no.'

"You're serious?" His voice trembling.

"Yes, I am. I know what happened to you was terrible, Elliot. You need help."

"I guess you're saying I'm crazy, huh?"

"Don't look at it that way. You experienced a lot of trauma. Seeing your brother get killed, most of your family died, and your future father-in-law killed your parents. You need professional help, baby."

"So, are you saying if I don't accept your ultimatum, then you're done with me for good? Is that what you're saying?"

He's getting upset. Pacing back and forth. Face tight. Fists clenched.

"Elliot, look at me, baby." He turns to face her. His eyes softened; tears flowing.

"I will wait for you no matter how long it takes. I will wait for you, baby."

"You promise?"

"I promise. Check yourself in. You don't have to go to the facility here. I heard there's an awesome clinic in Maryland."

"But that's so far away." Elliot complained.

"That's all right. Please go, and we can get married right after you complete the program."

"You promise? Don't lie to me, Rayna?"

"I'm not lying. I promise."

He hugs her and kisses her neck...softly, and gently. "I'll do it, Rayna. You wait for me."

"I will, baby. I will."

"Maryland, huh? I'll check it out. You want something to drink?"

"Yeah, a glass of wine, please, and thank you." He walks into the kitchen and sees the red gift box and envelope. He sees that the gift hasn't been opened. He fixes the drinks and brings the gift to her. "I see you haven't opened your birthday gift, beautiful."

"Elliot, I was afraid because I didn't know the man that dropped it off."

"I wasn't sure if you would accept it from me, so I hired someone to bring it."

"Wait! This is for my birthday?"

"Yes. You see, even without your ultimatum, I had decided to check myself in somewhere. I knew I wouldn't be here for your birthday so, I went ahead and got it."

"Oh, Elliot! I love you so much."

I put it on and modeled it for him. We drank our wine, watched a movie, and fell asleep holding each other.

CHAPTER 26

BEARER OF BAD NEWS

"Good morning, Mr. and Mrs. Brown. I'm Dr. Henry Newman."

The neurosurgeon seems disappointed and turns to Raymond, "I'm sorry Mr. Brown but your MRI results show a medium pea-sized mass on your brain. We need to take you down to get a small tissue sample in the morning."

"Oh no!" Tasha bursts into tears.

"Mrs. Brown, we will do all we can. We'll take the sample. Whether malignant or benign, we'll see what the best treatment options will be for him."

Raymond looks very worried now. "Is it going to be painful doctor?"

"No. You will be given a general anesthetic and won't feel a thing," he smiles, "As a matter of fact, we're going to do a neuro endoscopy where we take an endoscope to remove samples of tissue from the fluid-filled spaces in the brain. Here are some brochures you both can read tonight to give you a better understanding of what to expect before, during, and after the procedure."

Tasha takes them. "Is it terminal doctor?"

"Mrs. Brown, we don't know yet. We will find out after we take the tissue sample.

Raymond's mass is located in the pineal region of his brain which is in the middle of the brain right behind the brain stem."

"Do you think that's causing my headaches and stumbling, Doc?"

"Raymond, it could be. I mean, headaches and unsteady gait are part of the symptoms given the position of the tumor. Look, we'll take the sample in the morning and take it from there. Good night, folks and, see you in the morning at 8:00."

"Okay, thank you, Dr. Newman," Tasha said kindly. When he left, she rushed to Raymond's side and hugged him. She began to cry, "Oh baby, I love you so much."

"It's alright, sweetie. He said it's probably not cancerous. It's going to be fine. I feel it. I remember that the scripture says, 'If you have faith the size of a grain of a mustard seed, you can say to this mountain move from here to there, and it will move.' I believe in God, Tasha and, I believe His Word."

"It makes me feel better that you're putting your Bible to use."

"I read it every day. I guess now I have to apply HIS Word and see what happens." He strokes her hair away from her face. "Are you spending the night here?"

"Yes. I'm not leaving you. I will go home tomorrow and change after I find out what Dr. Newman says."

They finally fall asleep.

The next morning, Tasha is startled by the fluorescent light while Raymond is still snoring.

"Rise and shine you two. It's time to get dressed so I can take him down."

"Okay, can you give us fifteen minutes?" Tasha asked while yawning and stretching.

"Sure. My name is Jonathan."

"Thanks, Jonathan," Raymond said reluctantly.

Tasha helped Raymond put on a fresh, clean gown and the orderly came in to take him down to the operating room.

Tasha went to the waiting room and called her parents to give them the details about Raymond and to check on the kids. Her parents let her know they were praying for Raymond.

The kids were giggling in the background. It sounded as though they were having a great time. Tasha let them know that when their Dad is feeling better, they will be home.

As soon as she hung up, Raymond's cell phone rang.

"Hello?" Tasha answered.

"Hello, can I speak to Daddy, please?"

"Rayna?" Tasha sounded surprised. "Are you, Rayna?"

"Yes. Are you, Tasha?"

"I am. I'm glad you called. I'm sorry it's under these circumstances," she said quietly.

"What do you mean, 'under these circumstances'?" Rayna sounded frightened.

"Your father is not well and is in Kelton Memorial Hospital."

Now Rayna is upset. "When were you going to tell me? After he was dead?"

"No, dear. I was going to call you after the neurosurgeon let us know about the brain tumor."

"Brain tumor! Look, I want to see him. I'm coming. I will be there by 5:00 this afternoon. I just got off work and have to rest. Will you please inform me of any ***danger*** he may succumb to?"

"I apologize for not calling you sooner. Please forgive me. I will let him know you're coming when he comes out of recovery. I'm sorry if I upset you."

"Forget it! I will see you both this afternoon," and hung up.

In her mind, Tasha thought, "Oh, Lord, I think we just got off on the wrong foot."

CHAPTER 27

SURPRISE CALL

"Hello?"

"Hello. Hey, sorry about that. I was packing."

"Packing for what?"

"I'm going to do some soul-searching and traveling for a year. Man, she trying to send me to some rehab. Talking about 'you need professional help, Elliot.'"

"Oh yeah?"

"Look! I'm worth nearly 25 million. Who is she to tell me what I need? I can have who and what I want."

"I know, right? So why her?"

"Just because I can and her Daddy is responsible for my parent's death."

"Oh, word?

"You think I'm going to let that go?"

A computer chair suddenly went flying across the bedroom and smashed into the wall leaving a hole. Elliot is enraged.

"What's that noise, man? Sounds like somebody breaking in. You okay?"

"Yeah. You got everything in place?"

"Of course, I set up a couple of cams outside her place today. You sure you wanna go through with this, Elliot?"

"I want to know her every move," Elliot replies sneakily. "Thanks for placing the tracking device in her ring."

"Yeah, I hear you. Just make sure you deposit that $100,000 in my offshore account."

"Already done, bro.   Already done. You didn't give her your name when you dropped off the gift, did you?"

"Nah, man, I followed the script. I tell you this much though; man, she is a beauty!"

"Watch your mouth before *you* wind up missing!" Elliot punches the mirror.

"Calm down, fool! I was just giving you a compliment about your woman."

"I don't need your compliments; just do the job you paid to do before you get it."

"Listen bro, this my last job for you. I'm moving on to the Bahamas. I've got half a mil saved, I'm set. When I place this last cam at her Grandma's, that's it. I mean it, Elliot. I've helped you by illegally installing surveillance equipment, but that's it. Your Auntie's drowning and that fire was all you. I'm serious. Lose my number after this. The money was great but you went too far when you threatened me. You better think twice because if anything happens to me the Kelton PD will get a lot of evidence. Trust me; everything going viral. And another thing bro...rehab might not be a bad idea. Later."

Elliot's face cringed as he ransacked his bedroom like a roaring tornado. He started yelling and screaming inside his Charlestown penthouse, "Stupid ***Drake Hudson***! When his football career didn't work out and he was down on his luck, who gave him those hefty allowances to install the cameras? I did! Yeah, I took care of Aunt Trudie and them lying cousins all right. I warned them that they would have their *'part in my lake of fire.'* Uncle James had to suffer losses like I did. Sending me away to that rotten foster home. ***Vengeance is mine!*** I don't need Drake to get what I want done. I can do it myself! You watch me, Rayna Jennings! You're my ace in the hole to punish your father!"

CHAPTER 28

SIERRA MEETS BENJAMIN

"Hey, Ray-Ray. You made it back from Kelton yet?"
"Yeah, I got home a couple of hours ago.
"So, how'd it go?"

"Girl, that nosy Grandma went and told Daddy everything about what happened between me and Elliot. I'm so mad at her right now, Sierra."

"You know she means well, Ray-Ray. Don't take it out on her. Did that fool really leave for rehab?"

"Please, Sierra, don't start. He left last week. He already gave me my birthday gift since he can't be here. A ruby ring and matching earrings!"

I proudly hold it up to the light. I just love the sparkle!
"Well, excuse me," Sierra said mockingly.

"Girl, I can't wait until you get bitten by the love bug."

"Nah, sistagirl. I'm too ambitious and independent to be tied down. You know most men don't like that."

"That's just a cop-out, girl. I'll find someone for you."

"No thanks. It'll be just my luck they'll be like that crazy fool you got!" Sierra laughs, "Look, I've got to head to the grocery store. I'll talk to you later."

"Okay, sis."

Since she's trying to eat healthier, Sierra went to the *Whole Foods Market*. As soon as she walked in she heard, "Clean-up on Aisle 10," someone said over the intercom. Sierra peeped over and saw it was the pasta and sauce aisle. A muscular-built, average- height, clean-shaven bald man with a '*James Harden*' beard was apologetic and tried to help the employee clean up the mess.

"He's cute," she thought to herself and quickly walked past. She made her way over to Aisle 12 and chose a spicy salmon avocado roll and a thin-crust veggie pizza.

While she was trying to figure out which wine she should drink with her meal, someone stood beside her and said, "I like white wine myself."

Sierra does as well, but purposely chose the red wine and slightly glanced over at the gentleman next to her. Noticing that it was the "clean- up guy" from Aisle 10, she walked away.

"Hey, excuse me, pretty lady," he followed suit, "do you think you and I can share that?"

"I sure don't, stalker!"

"Nope, it's Benji; not Stalker," he said sarcastically.

"Excuse you? Like, the *dog*?" Sierra smirked.

"Oh, you got jokes. It's short for *Benjamin* and, I was just trying to be friendly."

Sierra didn't know what to say. She felt a little ashamed of herself. Looking up into those kind, hazel-brown eyes, she blushed and said, "My name is Sierra and, I apologize. I just got off work and I'm a little tired."

He quickly says, "Well, let me get dinner for you, Sierra."

"You're mighty stubborn aren't you, stalk—; I mean, Benji?"

They both laugh.

He smiles at her and says, "Sierra, a man has an eagle eye for inner and outer beauty. ***You***, my dear, are intertwined with both."

"Boy, you are smooth," she says shyly.

No man has ever made Sierra speechless, let alone, blush before.

Benji leans in towards her. "So, how about it? We can meet at the park if you like. Since we don't know each other well enough to go to our perspective places. I mean,."

Sierra felt flushed and confused. "Can you take my number and a raincheck? I don't feel up to a date tonight."

"Sure, that's fine. Can I call you tomorrow?" he said politely.

"Why tomorrow? What's wrong with tonight?" She sounded offensive and anxious.

"Well, I want to be respectful of your feelings. You said you were too tired for a date; therefore, you are probably too tired to talk. Get some rest. I will call you tomorrow."

Sierra truly admired not only his good looks but, also, his thoughtfulness.

After paying for their things, Benjamin walked her to her car.

As Sierra is driving away, she looks in her rearview mirror and he is waving with a smile from Earth to Heaven.

"What are the odds? I can't wait to call Ray-Ray," Sierra thinks to herself.

CHAPTER 29

RAYNA'S VISIT TO KELTON

It took me approximately three hours to get to Kelton Memorial Hospital. Upset with Tasha, Rayna kept thinking, "I can't believe she didn't tell me about my Daddy!"

Third floor, Room 315. *'Psyche Ward'*. I've got a few words for her. Why is my Daddy in a psychiatric unit?

"Hi, I'm looking for Raymond Brown. He's my Dad." Rayna said nervously.

"He's in Room 315. You can go on in. They will be bringing him up from x-rays shortly" The nurse replied.

His private room almost looks like a fanciful hotel room. Everything is so colorful and neatly placed.

Turquoise blue and grey walls with white wooden blinds and beach-themed paintings. Artificial greenery near his bedside. It seems cozy.

"I'm tired," Rayna said to herself. She sat in the over- sized recliner and fell asleep.

"Hello!" Tasha startled me by tapping my shoulder to awaken me.

"Hi," I said sleepily hoping there was no crud in my eyes or drool on my face. I sleep with my mouth open like Daddy. I got up and hugged him.

"Hey, Ray-Ray," he said surprisingly, "What are you doing here?"

"I came to see you! Tasha called and told me you have a brain tumor. What happened? Why are you in a psychiatric ward?"

I look up and Tasha is staring at me tight-faced. "What, heifer? Why you staring at me like that?"

"Look, he's going through enough right now. I would appreciate it if you would let him rest please."

"I don't need you to tell me what my Daddy needs. I just wanna know what's going on."

"Calm down ladies. Please." Raymond sounds agitated.

"You're right, baby. I'm sorry." Turning to Ray-Ray, Tasha quickly said, "I apologize to you too, Rayna. Your Dad tried to commit suicide a few days after his visit to see you. He was upset about your fiancée."

"Daddy, oh my goodness!" Rayna starts crying.

"Ray-Ray, it's not your fault, baby girl."

"Daddy, I'm sorry. I didn't know."

"It's okay," Tasha reaches out to hug Rayna.

"Listen, Tasha..."

Dr. Newman enters the room.

Tasha introduced me while I was still crying. She is so lucky because I was about to give her a piece of my mind.

"Hello," I manage to say.

Tasha gave me some tissue. I hesitated to take it from her except snot was streaming from my nose now.

"You're going to be all right, Raymond. Your tumor is not cancerous. I will schedule surgery for Friday at 6:00 a.m. to remove the tumor. You will probably remain in the hospital for three more days after surgery. I want to make sure it's safe for you to return home. Dr. Fitzgerald is coming around this afternoon for a visit.

Do you have any questions for me?"

"Doctor, what about Daddy's mental state? Is it safe for him to go home?" I asked.

"He was getting ready to be released after thirty days but the test results revealed the brain tumor. Dr.

Fitzgerald is his clinical psychologist and will be able to answer your concerns about his mental health. Here are some brochures of what to expect before, during, and after the surgery. Please feel free to contact me with any questions or concerns. See you Friday." He shakes Raymond's hand and gives Tasha and me a hug.

"Daddy..."

Raymond interrupted. "Wait, Ray-Ray."

He turned to Tasha and said, "Sweetie, I love you and appreciate you being here. I miss our babies and want to talk to them. If you don't mind please video chat them so they can meet their big sister!" He gives me a big smile. Tasha looks displeased but complies.

"Hi, Daddy and Mommy," the twins say with excitement, "We miss you. When are you coming to get us?"

"Real soon my hero and baby cakes!"

"Is that the nurse with Mommy?" Latisha asked. "No, baby cakes. This is your big sister, Rayna.

We call her 'Ray-Ray.' Would you guys like to meet her?"

"We have a big sister?" asked Anthony, "How cool is that? Hey sister!"

"Hey little brother and sister! I am a nurse; just not Daddy's nurse. I can't wait to meet you! What's your favorite color, Tisha and Ant-man."

They both laughed with excitement at my pet names for them.

"I like red," shouted Anthony, "and I like purple," said Latisha. I caught Tasha staring with a tight-muscled face as Daddy and I were ecstatically over the moon.

"Well, when I come for a visit, I have a surprise for you!"

They started singing and dancing, "We get a surprise, we get a surprise."

"Oh, you're both so adorable."

"They're not pets," I heard Tasha mumble under her breath. I ignored her. I was too excited to care.

"Okay, kids we will see you soon," Tasha told them, "Mommy and Daddy love you. Listen to Grams and Gramps, okay?"

"Okay, Mommy. Love you guys and you too Ray-Ray! Catch this!" and they blew a big kiss. We all pretended to catch it.

I was overwhelmed and began to cry.

"What's the matter, baby girl?" Daddy motioned for me to come to him.

"Oh, Daddy, thank you for including me."

"You're my baby girl. What do you expect?"

I turned to Tasha who was looking disinterested in my and Daddy's relationship and said, "Listen, Tasha, what do you say we start over? I think we got off on the wrong foot. I apologize if my presence annoys you or if you feel I'm overstepping my boundaries. I've been without Daddy for so long, and I'm glad he's back in my life. I don't want to lose him again. I can see that you truly love him and I'm grateful for that. Please let's both be strong for him to help get him through his mental crisis."

"You know what? You're right. I was a little jealous. I was on the defense because I was afraid you wouldn't like me or the kids."

"Are you serious? All I needed to know was that you love my Daddy. The fact that you're a nurse too is a bonus. I don't have to worry about his well-being."

Daddy was grinning with a smile from Earth to Heaven and hugged us both.

"This is the best time of my life right now ladies."

Dr. Fitzgerald entered the room and Tasha asked him to step into the hallway so she could catch him up to speed about Daddy's condition.

"Daddy, the twins are awesome. I apologize for the way I reacted towards Tasha. I had no right to be jealous."

"I know, baby girl. It's a lot to take in. I'm so glad you're here, but we have to have a serious talk Ray-Ray."

"Uh-oh."

Tasha and Dr. Fitzgerald come in and he says, "Raymond, I'm thankful they found the tumor and you're going to be okay. I'm going to increase your dosage of Risperdol and your therapy daily as needed. How are you feeling right now?"

"I'm okay. I don't feel stressed. I'm happy my daughter is here."

"Oh, hi, young lady," he reaches out to shake my hand and turns to Daddy, "Have you spoken to her about..."

"No, not yet. I was going to before you came in."

"What is it?" I was curious.

"Um. Well,."

"Just tell me, Dr. Fitzgerald. Please."

"It isn't healthy for Raymond to attend your wedding. Raymond has suffered traumatic experiences because of the accident and continues to need psychiatric care. I will have to advise against him going at this time; especially if you're planning to marry right away."

I looked at them with frustration and proudly said, "It just so happens that Elliot is going to therapy and rehab for a year at a center in Maryland. We will probably get married by my birthday next year."

"Well, that's awesome! Let's wait and see what happens then. I thought you were getting married this year by Christmas." Dr. Fitzgerald sounded elated and relieved at the same time.

"I'm sorry, Ray-Ray. You know I love you, but this is not just about the accident. I don't approve of this guy because he sounds a little disconnected. I probably have no right to say that given my condition. At least, I admit I have mental issues and am getting the help I need to get better. Your Grandma schooled me on what's been happening."

"That nosy Grandma. How dare she! I understand you want what's best for me. I get it, but I do love him and am going to marry him." I hug him and kiss him on the cheek.

"Oh, before I forget, baby girl, 'Happy Early Birthday'. I won't be able to come see you next month."

"That's okay, Daddy. You've both already given me two special birthday gifts."

I feel Tasha's genuine hug and concern as she says, "Just be careful about this guy, dear."

"Thanks. Tasha."

As I'm driving away, there's that feeling I'm being watched again. I look around but see no one. The hairs on my neck stand up. I realize I'm shivering and it's not because of the A/C either.

CHAPTER 30

DADDY'S RECOVERY

"Okay, Mr. Brown, it's time to take you down for surgery," the orderly said.

"I'm ready to get it over with. Tasha, please call Rayna and let her know how it goes, okay?"

"Sure, baby," she says as she kisses him gently on the hand, "God got you."

They smiled at each other as the orderly and nurse whisked him away.

Tasha decided to video chat with her parents while he was in surgery. They and the twins were so thrilled to see her.

Sounding concerned, her mom says, "You look tired, dear. When Raymond comes home, you need to get some rest. We should keep the children for a couple of more days when Raymond returns home. We're going to pick up more clothes for them."

"Awww, we appreciate you so much, Mom and Dad. I met his daughter, Rayna. She's nice and can't wait to meet the kids. She's also a nurse." Tasha sounded proud.

"That's awesome, dear," her mom said, "I'm glad things are working out."

Dr. Fitzgerald walks in with two cups of coffee and a smile from Earth to Heaven.

"Mom and Dad, I have to go. I will talk to you after Raymond's surgery and recovery."

"Okay, sweetie."

He hands her a cup of coffee and says, "I thought you'd like some coffee and conversation. No strings attached, okay?"

"Of course not."

He looks frustrated when he sees some pamphlets of various clinical psychologists in the area and says, "What's all this?"

"Well, Raymond and I have decided to switch to another psychologist," Tasha says sternly, "Thank you for your services, Dr. Fitzgerald, but we want to move on. We have already made the final payment to your office today. We were going to write you an appreciation letter, but saying it to you in person is even better."

"I admit I made a mistake, Mrs. Brown. I apo—-"

"Yes, you did." She said before he could finish. "You picked the wrong woman who cares everything about God, her husband, and marriage. If you think I'm going to let somebody like you separate my love from God and my husband, you got another thing coming. That energy you were trying to spill into me, you should pour into your wife. Did you bring her a cup of coffee this morning?"

Angrily, he hurled his cup of coffee into the trash and stormed out.

Another couple of hours went by as Tasha was anxiously waiting. She went to the hospital cafeteria to get some lunch. By the time she arrived at the room, Dr. Newman was patiently biding his time.

Panicky, Tasha asked, "Is everything all right?"

"Yes, the surgery was a success. He's in recovery now, and we were able to get the tumor."

"Praise Jesus!" Tasha cried out and lifted her hands toward Heaven.

Dr. Newman confirmed with an "Amen."

She shook his hand, gave him a quick hug, and called Rayna.

"Hello, Tasha," I answered immediately.

"He's going to be fine. They got the tumor, praise Jesus!"

"That's awesome! Is he out of recovery yet?"

"Not yet. Um, we are looking into finding him another psychologist besides Dr. Fitzgerald. Raymond deserves the best care from someone who can give him what he needs."

"Well, Tasha, my best friend is a clinical psychologist. I can ask her for some recommendations."

"That would be great, Ray-Ray!"

"Hey, Tasha, do you think I can visit my brother and sister on my birthday? It's—-"

"September 3rd!" Tasha interrupted with excitement. "And yes, Your Dad and I would love it as well. He should be feeling better then."

"Thank you, Tasha. This means a lot to me."

"You're welcome, sweetie. Oh, they're wheeling your Dad in. He looks a little groggy. Is it okay for us to call you tomorrow?"

"Yes, that's fine by me. Bye."

Raymond was mumbling, "C-Carol?"

"I'm Tasha!" she grimaced."

Still dazed and confused, Raymond said, "Come hold me, baby. I need you."

Tasha mumbled, "Which one? Me or Carol?"

"Tasha, come here, baby!" She complied and gave a fake smile; trying not to show how upset she was.

"We are going to have a serious talk," she thought to herself.

Chapter 31

TO SWEET FRIENDSHIP

"Hello, how are you?"

"Hi, Benji!"

"Someone doesn't seem so tired anymore. You didn't drink the whole bottle did you?"

Sierra laughed and said, "Only half of it."

"So, what are you up to, besides talking to me right now."

"I just finished tidying up the place and was getting ready for my morning jog."

"That explains that beautiful shape you have."

Sierra blushed, "Do you come off this sweet to all the ladies?"

"I plead the fifth."

"So Benji, tell me about yourself."

"Ladies first." he said wittingly.

"Okay. You already know my name. I'm a clinical psychologist at Sumnerfield's Recovery and Rehabilitation Center for Addicts. I—"

"Really?" he interrupted abruptly, "My Dad is in there. He may be your patient. James Nolan, Sr."

Sierra is startled. "Pastor Nolan's your Dad?"

"Yes. You know him?"

"I know of him. He was the guest pastor at my church a few months ago. My cousin is dating his foolish nephew, Elliot Nolan."

Benjamin sounded confused. *"Elliot Nolan*? I've never met him and Dad never mentioned him to me."

"You mean you've never met or heard of your cousin, Elliot? And James Nolan, Sr. is your Dad?"

"No, to the first question," he said uncomfortably, "and yes, to your second one."

"That's strange," Sierra said in her detective's voice, "I wonder why he hasn't mentioned him to you."

"Why did you call him a *'fool'*? Elliot, I mean."

"Because of the way, he's always busting up furniture and walls. He gets angry at the drop of a hat. I don't feel Ray-Ray is safe with him. No offense."

"None taken. As I said, I don't even know the man. Who is Ray-Ray?"

"My best friend and sister from another mister. It's Rayna but, we call her 'Ray- Ray'."

Benjamin became quiet for a second. "I'd like to get to know you."

"You are so sweet. Are you truly a person or an alien?"

"I confess I'm the latter. I come in peace," he said with a robotic-like voice.

They burst out with laughter.

"Seriously, I want to get to know you. Tell me more, Sierra."

"Let's see. I went to Chicago State University because that was my grandmother and mother's alma mater. My grandmother was a Professor in Abnormal Psychology and my mother was a psychiatrist. I love studying the brain.

Learning about the minds of people. Studying about why people think and act the way they do."

"Well, Queen, I wouldn't care if you probed my mind."

"Oh, I am."

"What do you feel or think of me?"

"You have a kind heart, Benji. I see it in your eyes. There's been a lot of pain...hurt."

"Yeah, I lost my mom to breast cancer a few months before my eighteenth birthday which is September 3rd. I was also in a toxic relationship for a couple of years that ended a year ago. Too many mind games."

"So sorry to hear that. That's tough."

"I lost my parents in the same year when I was twenty. My dad was a long-distance truck driver and fell asleep at the wheel. His truck exploded. My mom committed suicide about six months later. I think she grieved herself. I receive counseling for it, and I'm on medication for depression and anxiety. I hope this doesn't freak you out and you think I'm crazy."

"No, not at all," he said with relief, "I was going to let you know that I take medication for anxiety and depression. I had difficulty accepting Mom's death. I blamed Dad because I felt his absence caused her stress and cancer. After all, she was in love with him all those years. I thought he abandoned us until my Grandmother explained that she and Granddad didn't accept interracial marriages back then."

"Good to hear that we're both getting help. You say your birthday is September 3rd, huh?"

"Sure is?"

"Ray-Ray's birthday is September 3rd too."

"Should I take that as a good sign?"

"Of what?" Sierra said flirtatiously.

"This sweet friendship. See where it takes us?" Benjamin flirted back.

"Sure. Why not? I ain't got nothing to lose."

"Does it bother you that I live in Charlestown?" Benjamin asked sounding worried. "It's not that far away. About a forty-five-minute drive."

"No, it doesn't bother me at all."

"Good, Can we meet at Sumnerfield Park tomorrow for dinner and a walk? I'm versatile and have no food allergies."

"Me either. At what time?"

"It's a Saturday. Let's say six-thirty?"

"Perfect." Sierra's contemplating on where they should eat when...total silence.

"Hello?" Now Benjamin's nervous.

"Oh, I'm still here. I was just thinking of a restaurant on the riverfront. How about Ol' Jerry's Seafood? I can meet you there."

The night was restless. Saturday couldn't come fast enough for Benjamin. He felt Sierra was so easy to talk to. So different from his previous relationship with the older woman.

All morning that Saturday, Sierra had a nervous stomach. She couldn't believe she was running around like a high school teenager. Trying to figure out what to wear. Getting her nails done and a facial.

She had called Rayna and gave her all the details including about Elliot.

"I'm so proud of you, Sierra. He sounds like a nice guy."

"I believe he is, Ray-Ray. You know he's never met Elliot and said he's never heard of him?"

"I wonder why Pastor Nolan didn't tell him. You know Elliot has never mentioned Benjamin as being part of his family either?"

"I tell you, Ray-Ray, this is strange. Look, don't worry about it. I'm sure Pastor Nolan has his reasons. I have to get ready now. I will let you know how it goes.

Oh, you and Benji share the same birthday, how weird and exciting is that?"

"Speaking of which, Sierra. I'm glad you mentioned that. I'm going to have to cancel our outing because I'm going to see Daddy and my sister and brother for my birthday. I'm bringing each of them a surprise stuffed animal; one red and one purple. I'm so excited, Sierra!"

"As you should be. I'm happy for you. And no worries Ray. If all goes well with Benjamin and me, hopefully, he and I will go somewhere for his birthday."

"All right now. Bye, girl; have fun."

Driving his black cruiser, Benjamin arrived at the restaurant ten minutes early wearing his black cowboy hat and black leather boots with jeans, and a blue and black plaid collar shirt.

The closer it came to six thirty, the more Sierra's hands sweated. Benjamin was speechless when she arrived at the restaurant wearing her bell-bottom jeans and wedges with a pink-collar crop top.

They both ordered drinks and sat outside at the picnic table. They talked and laughed for about thirty minutes before he ordered a seafood boil upon Sierra's request.

It was a lovely evening as they sat by the riverfront and shared stories of each other's childhood. Sierra enjoyed listening to how he was raised by his single mom and having to take care of her when she was sick. He even showed her from his phone some of the buildings he designed in Charlestown and abroad throughout the United States. Even a couple of buildings in France.

As they took a walk around the park, Benjamin said, "I have a birthday coming up and would be honored if you would accompany me on a date if you don't have any plans."

Sierra smiled from Earth to Heaven. "It just so happens that Ray-Ray canceled our plans for her birthday, so I'm available."

"Awesome! I will let you know the details later."

Standing up and helping her from her chair, he says, "I'd like to walk you to your car if you don't mind."

"Sure."

Benjamin made Sierra feel like a Queen. Before you knew it, they were both holding hands as they strolled towards Sierra's car.

He leaned over and kissed her softly on the cheek. He took a bow and said, "Good night, me lady," and opened her door for her.

Sierra looked into his enchanting hazel-brown eyes and asked, "Call me?"

"You bet." He winked.

CHAPTER 32

"HAPPY BIRTHDAY, RAY-RAY"

"Happy 23rd birthday, Ray-Ray. I love you!"

"Thank you, Grandma. I love you too."

"So what are you going to do today? Do you want me to fix you some dinner since Elliot's away?"

"No, Grandma. I thought I wanted a party but quickly changed my mind. I'm going to see Tisha and Ant-Man today! I can't wait to spoil them and get to know them."

"Happy for you, Ray-Ray. What does Tasha think about all this?"

"She's all right with it...*now*. It was kinda rocky, at first, until we both realized all that matters is making Daddy happy and that we both love him."

"Awesome! Isn't it about a three-hour drive to Kelton?"

"Yes ma'am. I called them and told them how much I wanted to come and they agreed."

"What time are you leaving?"

"In about an hour. I will probably spend the night. I have to get back in time for work tomorrow."

"Okay, be careful, baby, and let me know you got there safely. Tell them I said, 'hello'. Love you."

Someone keeps beeping in. "Love you too, Grandma, and thank you."

"Hey, Sierra, I'm trying to pack."

"Happy birthday, sistagirl! What time are you leaving?"

"Thanks, sis. Um...in about an hour. Sorry, I had to break our dinner date. We can get together, on Saturday, if you are not too busy."

"Sure, that will be awesome and you can tell me about those '*lil boogers*'. Oh, Benji and I are going to hang out today. It's his twenty-seventh birthday."

"You sound a little *smitten*, diva."

"Shut up, Ray-Ray! You make me sick!" "It's all right, Sierra. I think it's wonderful!"

"Okay, but we're just friends. Taking things slowly, you know?"

"Yeah, I get it. I miss Elliot, but I'm excited I get to do this alone today."

"Whaaat? Loving that '*me-time*', huh?"

"Yeah, it gives me time to focus on myself."

"Good for you, Ray-Ray. Look, I don't wanna hold you up. We'll catch up. Love you. Let me know when you get there safely. I can't wait to meet my lil sis and lil bruh."

"All right. Thanks. Tell Benjamin I said 'Happy Birthday'!"

I hung up and went to grab the bowl from the console table to get my keys. What? Where are my keys? I remembered I made coffee earlier; maybe they're in there. Nope. I scanned the living room and there my keys sat on top of the mantle beside my snake plant. I could have sworn I left those keys in that bowl before I went to bed last night.

"Yeah, I'm getting older," I say to myself, "Thank you, Lord, for letting me see another birthday."

The twins are so excited to see me when I walk through the door and hand each of them their favorite-colored plushie. Tasha and Daddy welcomed me with open arms.

"Thanks for fixing one of my favorite meals, Tasha. Daddy must've told you how much I love cabbage lasagna."

"I must admit I was hesitant because I had never heard of it. I hope the kids like it."

"Mama used to fix it a lot." Tasha's face tightened. I quickly changed the subject.

"Daddy, what did the doctor say?"

"Well, I'm doing better since the surgery and they increased the dosage. I like the new psychologist Sierra hooked us up with. It's Dr....um, sweetie, what's the new doctor's name?"

"Dr. Aaron Makana, honey," Tasha yelled from the kitchen, I like him Ray-Ray. He's seeing Raymond Tuesdays and Thursdays and is on-call for him on the weekends."

"That's great! I told you Sierra knows her stuff. She's been at it for quite some time now."

"How's your Mama doing, Ray-Ray?!" Raymond asked.

"She's fine, Daddy." I glanced at Tasha whose eyes were filled with jealousy. I quickly steer the conversation while looking at the pictures in the photo album, "Tasha, are these the twins as babies?"

"Yes," she said with an enlightened tone, "They were about six months old there."

Tasha and I sat on the couch beside Daddy and 'oohed' and 'ahhed' over the twin's pictures.

"Hey, Rayna, come play with us," they happily interrupted.

I played with them for a couple of hours while Tasha prepared dinner. We played cops and robbers and built toy car models.

"Dinnertime, kids!" Daddy jokingly said.

We ran into the kitchen and washed our hands. The aroma of cabbage lasagna filled the air. I rubbed my belly and the twins mimicked me. We all laughed.

"I can't wait to sink my teeth into this! Thanks, Tasha." It tasted just as good as it looked and smelled. The twins dug right in. Surprisingly, they loved it! Ant-Man even asked for seconds. Tasha and Daddy were pleased.

I was stuffed but had to ask, "So, what's for dessert!"

"We made these chocolate chip cookies for you, Ray-Ray!" The twins said with excitement.

"Oh, thank you so much. How'd you know that they're my favorite?"

Tisha shouted, "Daddy told us."

I gave Daddy a big hug, "Ahh, you remembered."

"Of course, you're my baby girl."

"I'm your baby girl, Daddy," Tisha stomped her foot and rolled her eyes at me.

Daddy hugged her and said," Latisha you are my baby cakes and Ray-Ray is my baby girl, okay?"

Latisha looked at me confused and said, "But you're so old; you're not a baby!"

"Well, neither are you, lil sis." I smiled and tickled her.

She laughed so hard and hugged me and said, "I like you. You're a good big, old sister."

I said, "I'm going to get you for that!" I started chasing her around the kitchen table and Ant-man joined in. A pillow fight ensued in his room. I felt like a kid again.

This was so much fun.

"All right, kids. Settle down." Tasha and Daddy were standing at the door laughing.

This is one of my best birthday memories ever. I didn't want to leave that morning. The twins were begging me to stay as we shed tears.

Tasha hugged me and said, "Thank you so much for coming. Please let us know when you can come again. Maybe we can all take a trip somewhere when you have time."

"That would be nice." I hugged her and Daddy and left for home.

CHAPTER 33

IT CAN'T BE!

I was on my way home from Daddy's and realized I needed some gas. I was at the stoplight across from a Sheetz convenience store and someone pulled up beside me. By using my side view skills, it appeared to be Elliot's car.

"Is that Elliot? No way! He's supposed to be in Maryland at the rehab center.

As soon as the light turned green, I sped over to Sheetz. That car switched lanes and pulled in behind me. I jumped out of my car yelling, "What are you doing here, Elliot?"

"Uh, hi, baby. I was going to call you. I couldn't take it anymore, baby. I had to see you. I can't be away from you like that Ray-Ray! I love you." And before I knew it, he hugged me so tight. Kissing me gently on my neck.

"You called me '*Ray-Ray*!" I tried not to sound flattered.

"Wasn't it you that said, '*my friends call me 'Ray-Ray'*. I am your man...well, fiancé, right? Please, baby, it won't happen again. I need you. I'm going out of my mind without you. Please let me back in Ray-Ray."

He fell on his knees and grabbed me by the waist. He yelled out, "I love you, Ray-Ray! I messed up. I can't live without you. Take me back, please!"

An audience of spectators gathered and started clapping. Someone yelled out, "If you don't want him, I'll take him, girl."

"Well, you can't have him," I turned to her and rolled my eyes.

He quickly stood up and kissed me so tenderly on my lips. Everyone clapped and quickly dispersed as if they remembered why they had come to the store in the first place.

"Can I come home, baby? I want to move in with you."

"Not until we're married. You can spend a few nights though.

He was holding me ever so tightly now. It's like he did miss me. I felt so special. He kept kissing my forehead and ear lobes. "Stop, Elliot," I said playfully...not wanting him to.

"I love you so much Ray-Ray!"

"Okay, Elliot. We can do this, right? No more fussing or fighting if we're going to truly do this."

"Baby, you're right. I was so lost without you these past few months and I'll do better and right by you. Why don't we get married on Thanksgiving Day? That way we will always be thankful for each other."

I gently held his face in my hands and looked deeply into his beautiful eyes. Something inside me says "Nooooo!" But I see how serious about this he is. He seemed so different. Maybe the separation did us both some good. And without thinking, I said, "Yes, yes, yes! Let's do it."

"Great! I hope you don't mind but I want to go to the Justice of Peace and I want your Dad and Mom there. I want to prove to him that I forgive him."

"Justice of the Peace? Are you kidding me? Uh, I would rather have a shotgun wedding at the church than..."

"I said I forgive your Dad for taking my parents from me."

His face was tense. I see he's upset.

"I know, I'm sorry baby. Thank you for forgiving my Daddy."

"You drive me crazy, girl, you know that?" Then he leaned over and kissed me.

As we each drove back to Sumnerfield, I thought, "If he sold his estate in Kelton, then what was he doing there?" I can't help but wonder if Elliot is spying on me.

Where did he come from? How did he know I was in Kelton? I may have to get Grandma to hire Grandpa Harry's friend again.

CHAPTER 34

GRADUATIONDAY!

"Grandma, do you want to ride with me and Elliot or are you going to drive yourself?"

There's no answer. "Grandma?"

"I'm here, Ray-Ray. I don't see why he has to go to this. He should be in rehab himself."

"We have already had this discussion, Grandma. He's going to be my husband soon anyway. Everyone just has to get used to it."

"So you say, Lil girl."

"I'm not a little girl anymore. Are you going to ride with us?"

"No, I don't think so. Carol's going to ride back with me and then we're going to the park."

"Okay, Grandma. Love you."

"Love you too, Ray-Ray."

Elliot comes out of the bathroom and sees I'm in deep thought.

"Earth to Rayna!" He waves his hand in front of my face. I jump.

"What are you doing, Elliot!?"

"Nothing baby. I was just trying to get your attention. You were daydreaming. Is everything alright?"

"Yeah. Grandma just wondering if you should be at Mama's graduation."

"What do you think? Your thoughts are all that matter to me."

"Look, you are *my* man and I want you by my side.

We are soon to be married and they are going to have to get over it."

My phone rings and Elliot grabs it to answer.

"Hello?"

"Excuse you, fool? Where's Ray-Ray?" Sierra says angrily.

He rolls his eyes and tosses me the phone. I barely caught it.

"Hey, girl."

"So he's screening your calls now, Ray-Ray?"

"C'mon, Sierra. Gimme a break."

"What time are you leaving? Benji and I will meet you there."

"Okay. We're leaving in five minutes. See you."

As soon as I hung up, Elliot's face tightened and he rolled his eyes at me. "Some things are going to change when it comes to me and you. I'm tired of that *'so-called'* friend of yours."

"Ah, come off of it, Elliot. I'm sick of everyone trying to tell me to choose. Sierra's my best friend; my sister. She's got to get used to sharing me, that's all."

"Well, you already know I don't wanna share you with anybody."

He's angry now and slams himself onto the bed. I quickly sit down beside him.

"Look, there's no need to be jealous of Sierra or my family. No one is going to separate us. Only you can do that."

"Now what is that supposed to mean?"

"I told you, Elliot, if you start with those outbursts and breaking things, then I'm not going to be a part of your life."

He saw that I meant it and hugged me. "I'm never going to hurt you like that again, baby."

I look at my watch. "Oh my goodness! We need to go!"

Reluctantly, Elliot follows.

When we arrived, Grandma was waiting for us outside. I can tell she didn't truly want to but hugged Elliot anyway. When we got inside, Benjamin and Sierra met us in the foyer.

"Hi, Benjamin," I said and turned to Elliot to introduce them.

"Benjamin this is my future husband in a few weeks, *Elliot Nolan*."

Benjamin looks confused and turns to Elliot, "So you're my cousin?"

"Excuse me? Your what?" Elliot seems intense.

"If everyone will please take your seats. The ceremony is going to begin in ten minutes," Counselor Troy said over the mic.

Grandma went on in while Elliot was staring at Benjamin as though he wanted to punch him. Sierra and I looked on puzzled and couldn't figure out what to say.

Finally, Benjamin decides to break the ice and sticks his hand out to Elliot for a handshake. "Hi, I'm James Nolan, Sr.'s son. I didn't know he had any other family after what happened."

"Yeah, same here," Elliot said resentfully and shook Benjamin's hand.

"Um, maybe after this all of us can get together at the park. Okay, man?" Benjamin suggested.

Elliot appears annoyed but says, "Sure. That's fine."

Sierra and I glanced at each other and smiled. We all went in and sat down in the seats Grandma saved for us. The graduates were marching in now and I saw Mama anxiously searching for me and Grandma. We both waved to her. Benjamin and Sierra stood up to wave at Pastor Nolan. Elliot didn't move. He was filled with anger now.

After the ceremony, Grandma and I ran to hug Mama, and Benjamin and Sierra ran to Pastor Nolan. Elliot didn't move. Fist clenched; face tight.

"I'm so proud of you, Carol, and so is your Daddy." Grandma starts crying. "I knew you would do it someday. I prayed to God for many years about your deliverance."

Mama started to cry and hugged me and Grandma. "Thank you, Lord," she said.

I caught Mama glancing over at Pastor Nolan and smile. He smiled back and winked at her. I looked in Elliot's direction where he was sitting, but he wasn't there.

I start walking towards the foyer, "Mama...Grandma, I will meet you outside."

"Okay, baby."

I went outside to find him. He was nowhere to be found and the car was gone! I called him but no answer. Embarrassed and frustrated, I went back inside.

"Girl, what's wrong?"

"He left, Sierra! Elliot's gone!"

She looked around the room for Elliot. "Don't worry about it, Ray-Ray. He's probably upset finding out that Benjamin's his relative and that Mr. James didn't tell him."

"I suppose you're right. I guess he needs some time to himself."

"Did you call him?"

"Yeah, but he didn't pick up."

"What's going on?" Benjamin comes over. We fill him in and he says, "Well, I wouldn't worry about it. I mean it is strange the way we're finding out about one another. I was hoping we could get to know each other. I will find out from Dad why he didn't tell me about Elliot."

Mama, Grandma, and Pastor Nolan are making their way outside. Mama and he seem to have a lot to chat about. She looks so happy. She has a certain glow about her.

I call Elliot again. This time he picks up. "I'm sorry for running out on you like that, Rayna. It's just that, I didn't know anything about him. Uncle James kept that from me and I will find out why. Will you come home, please? I need you."

"Okay, baby. I was going out to celebrate with Mama and Grandma, but I will have them drop me off instead."

"Thanks, it means a lot to me, my beautiful."

I walked over and told Sierra what Elliot said. Of course, she complained, "You know I don't know why that fool trippin', Ray-Ray. You want me and Benji to drop you off?"

"Nah, but thanks. I'm gonna get Grandma to drop me off. What are y'all doing this evening? Or is that 'grown folk's business'?" I smiled.

"We're going to take Mr. James out to eat and then drop him off at the hotel. Benji is going to take him back to Kelton in the morning. He wants to take me to his place to watch a movie." She said candidly.

"Don't he live in Charlestown?"

"Uh, yes. I'm spending the night in his guest room."

"Yeah, right," I say in disbelief, "you sure you're not going to give away your cookies?"

"I'm not trying to rush, Ray-Ray. I want to be sure. And no offense, sis, but I'm praying about him first. And believe it or not, he's been the perfect gentleman. He hasn't tried to advance not one time." Sierra said proudly.

"How old is he?"

Sounding offended, Sierra said, "He's a man, Ray-Ray, unlike that dog in heat you're with."

"I'm sorry, Sierra. Calm down, *please!* Have fun." I hug her and wipe the egg from my face.

I found Mama and Grandma and let them know I needed to get dropped off. They were disappointed I wasn't going with them.

"Ray-Ray, for the last time, are you sure you want to marry that man?"

"Grandma, please. I love him and that's all that matters."

"Sometimes love is not enough, Ray. You need to ask God if this is who and what he wants for you."

Mama chimed in, "I love you, baby girl, no matter what you decide."

"I love her too, Carol. I just feel she's making a mistake."

"All right, love you guys. Sorry."

I say a prayer before I go in as they drop me off.

CHAPTER 35

SHALL WE CONTINUE?

"Thank you for that wonderful meal on the riverfront, son. I loved that rib-eye and baked potato."

"You're welcome, Dad. I'm so proud of you. It takes courage to do what you did. Get the help you need, I mean. You've inspired me."

"Well, son, It was a difficult decision to leave my flock to commit myself to rehab; nonetheless, I knew if I didn't, then I couldn't continue to lead. I've done some terrible things, Benjamin. I owe it to God to come clean and live out the rest of my days at peace with Him."

"Speaking of which," he interrupted, "Why didn't you tell me about my cousin, Elliot?"

James was suddenly overcome by fear. Astonished, he could not speak.

"Dad? Hello?"

"I'm sorry, son. It's a complicated story. Elliot's no good. I didn't want him to corrupt you and take you away from me, too. You're all I have left." James began to cry.

"Dad, no one is going to take me away from you ever. I love you. Sierra has told me how abusive and crazed Elliot can be. We're praying her friend doesn't marry him."

James is relieved and stops crying. "I understand Elliot's anger. He lost his parents in a car accident and I'm..." he starts crying again, "Oh no, Elijah...Elijah. Poor Elijah. I'm sorry. I'm sorry." He's sobbing uncontrollably now.

Benjamin seems confused even more now. "Who's Elijah?"

"Elliot's brother, son. I...I."

Immediately, Benjamin tries to console him. "Dad, whatever you have done, God forgave you for it and so do I. You don't have to give me details if you don't want to. Everything will be okay. I won't let anything come between us." Benjamin reassured him.

"Thank you, Lord. Thank you, son. It's been hard carrying this guilt...this burden for so long. God plus my therapist taught me how to release all my fears, my anger, my shame, and my grief. I confessed all my faults to God and He forgave me, son. He forgave *me*."

"Oh, I know about God and forgiveness, Dad. I forgave Mom and my grandparents for taking you away from me. Don't fret. I'll steer clear of Elliot."

"Okay, son. Love you."

"Love you, too, man.

James began to walk away.

"Hey, Dad, before you go. What did you mean that you didn't want Elliot to take me away from you, *too.*"

"Well, son," as he sighed, "I can't prove it, but I believe Elliot is responsible for the deaths of my family and that's why I was afraid to tell him about you. I had to protect you from Elliot because I don't trust him."

"You don't have to worry about that anymore from now on. I'm a grown man and can take care of myself. *Hakuna matata*, Dad, *no worries*, okay? Now, I'll see you later."

James wiped his tears and felt relieved that Benjamin finally knew about Elliot.

Finally home, James began cleaning up the kitchen when he picked up the graduation program on the table. He smiled when he ran across Carol Jennings' name and decided to call her.

"Hello, Carol. I hope I'm not bothering or interrupting you."

"Hi, James!" she sounded excited like a schoolgirl, "You're not interrupting anything. How are you?"

"Better...now that I'm talking to you. I was wondering if you would like to go to dinner?"

"But you live in Kelton."

"I know. I was planning on a getaway this Friday and coming back Saturday in time for church on Sunday. I like this steakhouse Benjamin and his girlfriend took me to on the riverfront in the park. Will you go, please?"

Carol suddenly became shy and speechless, "Sure, I will."

"Listen, Carol, I'm serious about getting to know you. I like you a lot."

"Hold your horses, James."

He replied with laughter, "Woman at both our ages, time is not on our side."

"Speak for yourself, James Nolan. I'm 35 and sticking to it. How old are you anyway?"

"I ain't ashamed of my age. I'm forty-five."

They both laughed as she said, "Well, you have me beat by five. You do the math."

"Age ain't nothing but a number, my sweet. Trudie was nearly five years older than me."

"Well, that depends on how you act. A lot of men still act their shoe size instead of their age and, I haven't seen a 45-foot shoe yet. Now, that said, you probably a 12 or 13."

"Touché. And the score is Carol, one...James, zero," he says jokingly, "So, Ms. Jennings, shall we continue?"

"Slowly, Mr. Nolan...slowly."

"So does this mean we are on for dinner Friday evening, my Queen?"

"I guess, Prince Charming." Carol chuckled.

"Okay, until then my sweet. This isn't good-bye but good-night," James said with a smile from Earth to Heaven.

"Good night!" Carol was ecstatic. "I hope this works out," she whispered.

"You say something, Carol?"

"No, Mama. Good night."

Chapter 36

"Elliot, I'm Home!"

As I tried to unlock the door with the key, it just opened with a push. "Elliot, I'm home!" The lights were off, except the light over the stove. To get to my bedroom, I used my phone as a flashlight. Elliot reeked of alcohol. I looked over at the nightstand and saw bottles of gin and vodka. He was passed out and must've forgotten to dress for bed.

"Oh well, so much for lovemaking tonight," I sighed. I took a shower to soothe my 'cookies' and went to bed.

The next morning I awoke to Elliot singing in the shower. He's handsome but certainly wasn't gifted with a singing voice. I opened the bathroom door and peeked my head in, "Good morning, baby."

"What are you doing in here, Rayna? You don't know how to knock?"

"Excuse you?, I said angrily. Then I noticed, "Ooh baby, what happened to your back? That's an ugly scratch. And your arm? What happened to you? Did you get in a fight?"

"Look, will you stop hounding me, woman? I'm all right. Will you just go and fix breakfast, please?"

"If we're going to be husband and wife, then we need to be transparent. Stop keeping secrets from me, Elliot."

"Ain't nobody got no secrets! They say the guilty dog always barks first. You're the only one barking about secrets and got the nerve to accuse me. What secrets you got, Rayna? Huh?"

I felt afraid all of a sudden. Thoughts racing through my mind. Did he find about me and Garrett? How I ran into him at the grocery store the night of our first date and had a quickie in that ol' raggedy pickup truck of his; listening to that stupid country music.

Slamming his fists against the shower tiles, he swiftly turned to me, "You hear me, Rayna?"

"Look, I don't want to argue with you. I think we're both a little tired and hungry. I will fix breakfast and then we will talk about our double date with Sierra and Benjamin this coming weekend."

"I ain't going around him or that heifer."

"Well, I will go without you."

"You would do that to me, baby? Leave me alone?"

He steps out of the shower and pulls me in. My 'cookies' remembered how much they liked his filling. He grabbed me and kissed me all over, including my 'cookies.' Guess I won't be going after all.

I started fixing brunch around 11:00 when Elliot and I began to discuss the wedding. "Baby, are you sure you want us to go to the Justice of Peace?"

"Yes, please. We will need to get ready for our honeymoon in the Bahamas. We're going to stay at the Atlantis."

"For how long? Because I will need to let my job know."

"At least a week. That's all the time I need."

"I've never been to the Bahamas before."

"I know."

"How do you know?" I said jokingly.

Elliot grabs me by my tiny waist and looks deeply into my eyes, "Trust me, baby. I know all about you." Then kisses me gently on the forehead. I want to ask him about those scratches again, but why ruin the peace right now?

Then I thought, "Nah, you don't know everything." For a split second, I think of Garrett.

There's Pastor Nolan's voice in my head again, "Pray before you do, dear."

I hold on to Elliot tightly as though I were seeing him for the last time.

CHAPTER 37

THAT'S STRANGE

"Hey, Sierra. Are we still on for today?"

"Sure. How are you, babe?"

"I'm doing okay, I think."

"What's up?" Sierra sounded worried.

"Well, I talked to Dad and he said the reason he didn't want to tell me about Elliot is that he suspects he killed Dad's family, but he can't prove it."

"Are you serious?"

"Yeah, I'm just as shocked as you are. Dad warned me to stay away from him."

"That fool. I need to tell Ray-Ray. I can't have her marrying that psycho. She's my best friend, Benji."

"I think we need to look into it first, sweetie. Let's get evidence for Dad's and Rayna's sakes. Okay?"

"But she's marrying him in a few weeks."

"Well, we better get started then. Do you know of any private eyes? I will pay for it."

"I will talk to Grandma Flo. She used a friend of Grandpa Harry's to find Ray-Ray's Dad. Um…David somebody. He's a retired cop."

"Okay, when I come over let's go see her."

Sierra's voice was filled with curiosity, "So, your Dad believes Elliot's responsible for the *entire* family's deaths?"

"Yeah."

"Let me call Grandma Flo to let her know we're coming over."

"Okay see you around 4:00."

Sierra was frustrated and relieved at the same time because her hunch about Elliot was spot on. She did have a slim glimpse of hope for Ray-Ray marrying him when he paid for the damages to her townhouse and got her that ruby ring. Sierra knew she had to get on the ball if she wanted to stop this wedding.

"Hello, Grandma Flo. I need a huge favor."

"Hey sweetie, what is it?"

"Benji wants to hire that private eye you used to find Raymond."

"That's strange."

"What's so strange about that?" Sierra inquired.

"Ray-Ray called me yesterday and asked for David to check on something about Elliot. She seems to think he's spying on her."

"What? He's psycho Grandma. We have to get Ray away from him."

"I know, Sierra. David and Ray-Ray are coming over around 4:30 today."

"Perfect! Benji and I will be there too."

"Okay, see you then."

When Benjamin finally pulled up, she practically met him in the car.

"Step on it, baby! The private eye is going to meet us at Grandma Flo's, she said excitedly. "And guess what?

Ray-Ray has her suspicions too. She wanted to hire him because she thinks Elliot is spying on her."

"Wow! What's the matter with my cousin?" "Psychotic, that's what."

Chapter 38

PRIVATE EYES

"Well, well, well. What do we have here? Now where do you think you're going, Rayna?" Elliot said gazing at his computer. He watched Rayna undress and step into the shower.

"That's right, my sweet. Eyes watching you." What are you going to wear today so I can match that outfit?"

Rayna gets dressed and slips on a sun-yellow t-shirt dress with cursive black letters "*Faith*" imprinted in the center and put on a pair of black sandals.

Elliot slips on a pair of black jeans and a sun-yellow shirt with yellow and black sneakers to match. "Now, let's see where you're going so I can show up too. You ain't doing nothing without me, beautiful. Oh, that's right. You've got to find those keys first."

Rayna grabs her black and yellow handbag and walks over to the bowl on the console table by the front door to get the keys. "Lord, where did I put my keys?" she mumbled.

Elliot snickers as he watches everything unfold from his laptop. "Keep looking, beautiful. You're getting close."

Rayna searches the bedroom again. Her purse falls from her shoulder to the floor. As she bends to pick it up, she notices a keyring peeking out from under the bed. "What in the world? How did you guys get under here?" She picks them up and goes on.

"That's good. Aren't you a smart one? You found them sooner than I expected. Let's see where that ring is going to take us," Elliot grins eerily.

"I'm running late, Grandma. I couldn't find my keys."

"Okay, baby girl. I don't know what's going on but Benjamin and Sierra are on their way over too. They want to hire David."

"What for?"

"I'll let them explain. They didn't tell me." Elliot follows the tracking device on the screen.

"Going to Grandma's are we?" He switches the cameras over. Nothing but static. He panics, "What? Where are the? What the?" He screams, "Drake, you double-crossing, backstabbing..."

Suddenly, furniture starts sailing through the air. Drake's phone rings.

No answer.

Elliot calls again.

No answer.

"You think you can take my money and get away with it. I'll kill you for this Drake. I will find you."

His phone rings.

"I thought I told you to lose my number, Elliot," Drake says angrily, "I'm done with you. I can only be charged with illegally installing surveillance. But you, well, you committed the murders. I had nothing to do with that. I have proof...and remember, it will go viral if anything happens to me *accidentally*. Now what do you want?"

"Look, I don't care. I'm going to kill you if I lay eyes on you, Drake. You know you were supposed to set up the cameras at her Grandma's house."

"I did set 'em up. I have proof, man...of everything!"

"But..." Elliot is flabbergasted.

"Hey man, they may be on to you. You betta get out. Leave before they catch up to you. Don't call me anymore. I'm getting rid of this phone and leaving the Bahamas. I'm out."

The phone goes silent.

"Drake? Hello?"

No answer.

Elliot starts screaming and punches the mirror. Throwing himself to the floor, he screams, "I will have *my* revenge."

The tracker ends at Grandma Flo's house. Elliot leaves Charlestown and heads for Sumnerfield.

CHAPTER 39

FINDING LOVE AGAIN

"I don't know why I'm so nervous. I haven't felt this way since I dated Raymond." Carol's phone rings and she anxiously answers without checking, "Hello, James. How are you?"

"I'm fine, Mama." I start laughing.

"Ray-Ray?" Carol sounded embarrassed, "Um...what's up, baby girl?"

"*James*, huh? You like him don't you Mama?"

"Girl, this grown folk's business. What do you want?"

"Well, I'm on my way to Grandma's to meet with that private eye to do some checking on Elliot before I marry him in about four weeks. I have to do a few errands first though."

"That's good. You can't be too careful these days. However, you don't want to wait so late and end up a bitter old maid. Remember, *a piece of a man* is better than *no man* at all."

"I hear ya, Mama. But I don't want to just settle either and *still* wind up a bitter old maid," I proudly say.

"Ray-Ray? Carol says with a serious tone.

"Yes, Mama."

"I think I'm truly fond of James."

"Mama, I think that's awesome!"

"He's coming to take me out to dinner on the river-front. Can you give me some pointers on what to wear? It's been a while since I've been infatuated with someone other than your Daddy."

I burst out with laughter, "Oh, you'll be fine, Mama. Just don't dress like you trying to give away your cookies or as a nun."

"Ray-Ray. You know he's a man of the cloth."

"Well, Mama it ain't like he doesn't need some too. Nah, I'm joking. You'll be fine. Just be yourself. Wear a nice blouse and some jeans with a pair of wedges. Is he in town?"

"Yeah, he's leaving Saturday evening to get back in time for his church service on Sunday."

"Mama, if you happen to talk to James can you not mention the part about the private eye, please?"

"Yeah, sure sweetie. I have to get dressed now. He'll be here soon. Love you. I'll tell you all about it."

"Okay, Mama. Love you too. Have fun."

Carol looks through her closet to find a white belle-sleeved blouse and a pair of ripped blue jeans. She thinks to herself, "I think I'll wear my black Michael Kors wedges. Glad I got my nails and toes done."

James calls Carol who answers right away, "Hi, James. How are you?"

"Fine, now that I hear your voice, beautiful lady. I'm pulling up in about ten minutes. Is it too forward for me to come knocking? I don't want to embarrass you in front of your mother."

"I wouldn't have it any other way. My mother likes you a lot. She would be happy to see you."

Carol smiles when she gets off the phone and finishes getting dressed. She hears a knock at the door while putting on her black earrings and takes a look out of her bedroom window.

She sees Benjamin and Sierra getting out of the car and thinks to herself, "We must be double-dating tonight." Then she feels disappointed.

"I'm coming," Grandma Flo yells from the kitchen.

She was making refreshments for her small group of guests. "Hi, you two. Come on in."

"Something smells good," Benjamin sniffs the air.

Grandma Flo proudly motions for him to come into the kitchen while Sierra takes a seat on the sofa. "It's just some buffalo chicken dip I made to go with these *Tostito* scoops. She grabs a spoon for him to do a taste test. "Do you like spicy or regular?"

"I like spicy with a strong kick." He smiles and sticks out his chest.

"All right. Here you go."

"Wow! This reminds me of the way my Grandmother used to make it."

"Good. Well, get on back to Sierra while I finish up. It'll be ready by the time Ray-Ray and David get here."

"David?" Benjamin inquires.

"Yeah, the private detective you and Ray-Ray hired. I'm glad y'all doing this and excuse me for talking about your family, but something's wrong with Elliot. There's something I found that I need to show y'all."

Carol enters the room and talks with Sierra.

"Hey Sie, how are you? Are y'all going with me and James tonight?"

"No, we are going to meet with the private eye about Elliot. You look great!"

"Y'all too!" Carol was relieved and tried not to allow her face to affirm it.

"Sierra, what in the world is going on? Should Raymond and I have someone to *'take care of'* this man? We still got street connections, you know."

"Nah. Not that serious. We just want to make sure Ray-Ray is making the right decision."

"Oh okay. She's hiring this private eye too? Y'all please keep me in the loop."

"We will. But look at you, diva." Sierra hugged her and whispered, "I'm so proud of you."

There's a knock at the door as Benjamin is entering the living room. "I'll get it."

"Thanks, 'cause I'm busy," yelled out Grandma.

"Dad?" Benjamin looked confused.

"Hi, son, what are you doing here?"

Sierra jumped up and quickly interrupted, "Benji and I were invited over to have refreshments with Ray-Ray and Grandma Flo."

Grandma came waltzing in and bluntly said, "Quit standing out there letting in mosquitos and letting out my air. Come on in Pastor!"

"Thank you, but call me *"James"* please; except when I'm in a church setting, of course."

Grandma felt embarrassed. "Okay, sorry," and everyone retired to the living room.

"So, where y'all headed? Grandma sounding nosy.

"Just to get some dinner at the park on the riverfront, Mama." Carol swooped in and slid her hand in James'.

"Yeah, we'd better get going Carol," James politely said while making his way to open the door for her. "Nice seeing you again, ma'am, and you too, Sierra. Son, we'll talk later, okay?"

"All right, Dad." Benjamin smiled with approval. "Have a good time."

While James and Carol were walking to the car, someone pulled up.

CHAPTER 40

AUNT HILDA MAE VISITS KELTON

"Hello?"

"Oh, hi, Aunt Hilda," Tasha says excitedly, "How are you?"

"Well, I'm fine. I miss y'all and was hoping to come for a visit. I haven't seen them babies in a while. That's all Ray-Ray talked about since she got back."

"Sure, that would be great. I'm sure Raymond would love to see you."

"Okay, don't tell him. I want it to be a surprise."

"If you say so. When are you coming?"

"I'm leaving now and should be there by noon. I want to go to Pastor Nolan's church Sunday morning. So can I stay with y'all?"

"Of course! You know better than to ask that. You are welcome here any time, Aunt Hilda."

"Not according to Raymond."

"Now that's not true and you know it." Tasha reassured her, "Just come on. We will be glad to have you."

"Well, see you."

Tasha looked over at Raymond who was sleeping peacefully on the couch. She didn't want to disturb him but knew it was best to let him know Aunt Hilda was coming. Raymond doesn't take kindly to surprises. They tend to overwhelm him; possibly upset him depending on the surprise.

The twins came racing into the living room to play tag and used their Dad as base. This startled him out of his sleep.

"What's going on kids?"

"Tag! You're it, Daddy!" Anthony and Latisha giggled.

Raymond was tired from the meds. "Kids, Daddy's drained. Can I sleep please?"

They were disappointed. "Ah, you're no fun, Daddy."

He jumped up and tickled them as they ran to Latisha's room. "No fun, huh? I'll show you." He pretended to karate chop her dolls then grabbed a pillow and started a pillow fight with them. Everyone was laughing when Tasha came to referee.

"Okay, kids, that's enough. Daddy and I need to talk for a minute. You two keep playing."

Raymond was relieved and kissed Tasha's forehead. "Thanks, baby."

"Uh, we do need to talk. sweetie."

He saw the concern on her face. "What's wrong?"

"Aunt Hilda is on her way here. I told her she could stay this weekend. She wants to go to Pastor Nolan's church on Sunday."

"C'mon, baby. Couldn't you tell her 'no'? She's always judging me. Nothing I do is ever good enough. I won't have her doing it to our kids. She's so negative all the time."

Tasha rubs Raymond's back to calm him. "Look, I will intervene if she oversteps her boundaries, okay?"

He starts rubbing his head as though he's agitated. "Lord, help me I need a drink."

"No, baby," Tasha hugs him, "I'll be right here with you every step of the way. I won't let her get out of line. I promise. Let's call Dr. Makana."

Raymond went into the bedroom and talked to Dr. Makana. He went over a few techniques and breathing exercises for him to cope. Raymond was calm by the time Aunt Hilda arrived.

Before Tasha answered the knock at the door, she took a deep breath and smiled, "Hi, Aunt Hilda, welcome."

"Hey, Tasha, you looking mighty plump, chile. Baby fat didn't go from you so easily, I see."

"You..." Raymond was about to chime in.

"You look great, Aunt Hilda!" Tasha exclaimed.

"Who is this lady, Mommy? asked Latisha.

"And Why does she look like a hippo?" Anthony asked.

"Latisha Rae, you apologize to Aunt Hilda right now!" Tasha was embarrassed. "I'm sorry, Aunt Hilda."

"It's okay," she turned to the kids and said, "This hippo's name is Aunt Hilda, and she's hungry."

They all laughed; especially Raymond who gave Latisha a high-five when she walked past him.

Aunt Hilda came in and sat across from him in the recliner. "So how are you, Raymond?"

"Doing fine, Aunt Hilda," he answered without looking at her.

"I see you put on some weight, she started nagging, "and when you gone cut that hair?"

"I'm not," he said calmly while turning his attention to the news.. "In fact, I'm a grown man, Aunt Hilda, and if

I want to grow my dreads past my knees, then that's my business."

She rolled her eyes, "Well, aren't we a bit testy today? Who peed in your cornflakes this morning?"

"I wouldn't know, I don't eat cornflakes," he said with a smile.

"Boy, you betta mind how you talking to me."

"Aunt Hilda you should mind how you talk to me; otherwise, you may find yourself at a hotel."

Tasha came in from the kitchen and overheard the conversation, "Hold on, honey. Aunt Hilda is family and will stay here as long as she **minds** her business."

Kneeling beside Aunt Hilda, Tasha says, "Look, I'm not sure why you've always talked down to Raymond, but it stops now. Today. Whatever animosity you have towards him, you need to fix it. You can't go to Heaven this way, Aunt Hilda. Not the Heaven you keep talking and singing about."

Aunt Hilda looked embarrassed and with tearful eyes said, "You're right."

Sitting beside Raymond on the couch, Aunt Hilda took a deep breath and held his hand. Seeing her weary, tear-filled eyes, he realized how much she had aged. He suddenly felt sorry for her. She began to cry and Raymond hugged her. He could feel her pain and cried too.

"I miss her so much, Raymond. I miss your Mama. Helen was my best friend. We were thick as thieves. I was even jealous when she married Frank. When they died, I couldn't take you at first because I had a nervous breakdown and started dabbling in drugs. I couldn't deal with it. I blame myself because I was too lazy to go to the store so I asked them to pick me up a loaf of bread and some chips from Cecil's." Then the robbery happened," crying uncontrollably, she said, "It's my fault, I'm sorry, Raymond. I'm sorry!"

Tasha gave her some Kleenex and sat on the other side of her. The kids ran into the room and she motioned for them to go play as Aunt Hilda continued to cry.

"We're hungry, Mommy," Anthony said.

Tasha speedily fixed the kids a plate of spaghetti, gave them some juice, and went back to the living room to comfort Raymond and Aunt Hilda.

Raymond was rubbing Aunt Hilda's hands. "It's okay, Auntie, let it out. It's not your fault. Losing your sister and my parents was a tough blow to both of us, but I believe you coped the best way you could. I know I didn't say it, but I appreciate you for taking me in."

Aunt Hilda looked at him with kind, sorrowful eyes. "I didn't treat you right a lot of the time Raymond because I never wanted children, and the crazy part is you look just like her. I am so sorry I resented you. I was so angry about Helen's death that I took it out on you."

She wiped away her tears as the twins ran into the living room covered in spaghetti sauce. Aunt Hilda grabbed them both and gave them a bear hug. "Didn't I tell y'all I was hungry? I'm going to eat you up." The twins laughed as she pretended to bite them.

Raymond and Tasha shared a smile and hugged her tightly.

"Okay, let's get you guys cleaned up. Raymond, can you fix a plate of spaghetti for Aunt Hilda, please?"

"Sure, baby," and he turns to Aunt Hilda and says, "Allow me to escort you to the kitchen, dear lady."

As she hugged him and put her hand in his, she said, "Forgive me, son. Can you recommend me to your therapist?"

"Yes, ma'am. I just talked to him before you came," he chuckled.

"I understand. I want to mend ways and make it up to you. I want to go to Heaven, Raymond. I don't want anything to get in the way of that. I believe God used Tasha to remind me of that. I haven't been feeling too well lately, and I have a doctor's appointment next week and want you to come with me."

"I'm grateful and all is forgiven. Let's not talk about it anymore, okay? I will be happy to come with you. Can Tasha come too?"

Aunt Hilda hesitated at first then said, "Yeah, I guess it'll be all right."

Tasha came into the kitchen. "Babe, you haven't fixed her plate yet?"

"Oh, my bad. We got distracted in conversation. Aunt Hilda wants to go to therapy."

"Really, Aunt Hilda?" Tasha exclaimed, "I know a great therapist for you! His name is Dr. Aaron Makana. He's excellent for Raymond."

"Yeah, I feel it's time. I need to finally deal with grief, getting older, and depression."

Raymond looked worried, "Depression, Aunt Hilda?"

"Yeah, Raymond. Now that I'm turning sixty-seven, I feel lonely and afraid. Most days I don't even want to get out of bed. I haven't even told Flo."

Tasha jokingly said, "Well, maybe when you go to Pastor Nolan's church on Sunday you'll meet a handsome gentleman."

"No thank you, dear," Aunt Hilda said abruptly, I've already had *a piece of a man* before. I'd rather be alone with my *peace of mind*. Many couples don't have something special like you two have or what Flo and Harry had. *Real love*."

"Okay, I'm sorry Aunt Hilda. I didn't mean to upset you."

"Oh, it's all right, sweetie. Do you think you can set me up an appointment with that doctor? I can't do it next Tuesday though because I have to go to my medical doctor. He wants to run some tests. I haven't been feeling well lately."

Raymond sadly looks over at Tasha. "Here Aunt Hilda sit down and eat. Tasha and I will get the kids ready for bed."

"If y'all don't mind, I would like to read the kids their bedtime story, please."

"We don't mind." Raymond smiled.

While they were getting the kids ready for bed, Tasha said, "Raymond, are you thinking what I'm thinking?"

"Moving her in with us?"

"Exactly."

It was Latisha who asked, "Who Mommy?".

"None of your bees wax, missy."

The bathroom flushed in the guest bedroom. Aunt Hilda Mae had finished her dinner. When she came out of the bathroom, she had on her bathrobe and silk bonnet. "Okay, who's ready for a bedtime story?"

"We are!" The twins burst with excitement.

"Anthony, you pick the story tonight, and Tisha, you can pick the one tomorrow night. Sounds fair?"

"That's fair," Tisha said.

"Go on Tasha and Raymond and eat your dinner. I can take it from here."

Raymond looked at the kids and then looked at Aunt Hilda Mae. He realized she meant what she said about making amends and they hugged the kids and went to eat.

During dinner, they agreed that they would talk to Aunt Hilda Mae about moving in with them after her doctor's appointment. They felt she shouldn't be driving long distances anymore either. Tasha tried to convince her to stay until Tuesday so that she could drive her to the doctor. Raymond suggested they take her to church on Sunday also.

CHAPTER 41

LET'S GET DOWN TO BUSINESS

James casually led Carol over to the passenger side of his silver *BMW* convertible to open the door when someone shouted out, "Carol? Is that you, beautiful?"

"Yes it is," James said calmly and reached out to shake the gentleman's hand.

Carol turned slowly and shrieked, "Oh my Lord, Mr. David!" and gave him a warm hug. "It's great to see you! How are you?"

"I'm doing well, young lady. I'm glad to see you are too," he turns to James shaking his hand, and says, "Take care of her young man. She's like a daughter to me."

James seemingly defensive says, "No worries, sir. I will."

Carol sensed his tone and held his hand while looking deeply into his eyes, "James, Mr. David is like a father to me. He has been here for Mama and me since Daddy died. He is Dad's lifelong friend as well as ours." She turns to Mr. David, "Thank you for coming to visit Mama. We'll talk soon, okay?"

"Sure, baby girl. Y'all enjoy your evening." Mr. David shakes James' hand again.

He knocked on the door and Grandma Flo opened up, "Hey, David!" She said as she hugged him. Everyone was seated except Rayna. "I'm getting ready to call Ray-Ray to see where she is," Grandma said while bringing out refreshments.

"I already did, Grandma. She's almost here. She said she had to run some errands."

Just then a knock at the door. "I'll get it," said Benjamin, "It's probably Ray-Ray now." He looks through the peep-hole and opens the door. "Elliot? What are you doing here, man?"

Sarcastically, Elliot says, "What's up, *cousin?* I can't come to see my future family. He brushes against Benjamin, slightly shoving him, "Man, step aside," and he walks into the living room.

Astonished, Grandma says, "Elliot, what are you doing here?"

"I came to see you and my future Mama-in-law. I also came by Rayna's and she wasn't home. I just figured she was here."

"You didn't call her?" Sierra asked sharply.

Elliot glared at her, "Why call when I can just come?"

Grandma butted in, "But Elliot, honey, this is my house and everyone knows you call me before you come, except Carol and Ray-Ray."

"Well, Grandma, I don't have your number."

"Which is why you should've called Ray-Ray and waited for her, fool." Sierra rolled her eyes at him.

Elliot says angrily as he steps toward her. "You know what, heifer, you're gonna stop calling me 'fool' and addressing me in that tone!"

Benjamin steps in Elliot's face, "Back off cuz. Don't step to my woman like that!"

"Hey! Everyone calm down and sit down," Mr. David stood up as if he were the man of the house. You could hear the authority in his voice. They all sat down, including Grandma.

Soon a key could be heard turning the door. Ray- Ray walks in just in time to witness the staring match between Elliot and Benjamin. "Elliot, what are you doing here?" she says nervously.

"Hey baby," he gives Benjamin a hostile stare once more and walks over to Rayna kissing her gently on the forehead. "I had to see you. We need

to talk."

"Okay, baby, but it's going to have to wait until I get back home. Can you wait for me there please?" She hugs him and kisses his cheek.

Elliot scans the room looking at everyone as he suspects something. "Why are you trying to get rid of me, Rayna?"

She steps back and notices they're dressed alike in sun yellow and black. "Well, well, I see we're twins again," she says with hopes to avoid answering the question.

He sees all eyes are on them. "It just goes to show you that great minds think alike. But you still didn't answer my question?"

"Um...what?

"Why are you trying to get rid of me?"

"Elliot, no one is trying to get rid of you. I didn't even know you were coming tonight. I had already planned this. I will see you at the house, okay, baby? Please." She leans over and whispers in his ear, "I'll give you some cookies and cream!"

"All right, I hear you. See you when you get there." He looks around at everyone and apologizes for the intrusion. He glances at Benjamin and says, "Later for you, cuz."

Benjamin stands up and says, "Believe it, cuz."

As soon as Elliot leaves, everyone breathes a sigh of relief.

"Talk about cutting it close," Grandma plumps down in her recliner and wipes sweat from her forehead."

Mr. David stands in front of the mantel with a notepad in his hand as if he's getting ready to give a speech, "Let's get down to business," he says methodically.

"Wait," Grandma scurries to the kitchen and comes back with a box.

David motions for her to place it on the floor nearest him. We look on with inquiring minds trying to discover what's in the box.

"Now, let's get down to business," David continues, "I have been checking into Elliot's past and found that he lost his parents around age 8 to a drunk driver named Jason Turner. Raymond was a passenger. Jason confessed before he died of cancer that he switched places with Raymond and left the accident. He knew that if he hadn't, then he was looking at life in prison."

I began to cry and Sierra gave me some tissue. I was so relieved and couldn't wait to tell Daddy and Elliot the good news. Wait! I haven't heard all the details yet!

David got on with it. "Elliot is still under investigation for the deaths of Trudie, James Jr., Kayla, and Kristen Nolan. Authorities can't prove it but believe he is responsible for their deaths. He has alibis for the timing of their deaths. However, I have one lead that will cause me to go out of the country for a few weeks." He looks at me and reiterates, "Do **not** marry him just yet, Ray-Ray."

"But if he has alibis and they can't prove it, I think he's innocent. All I see is a man who has suffered many tragedies in his life and needs psychological help."

"Ray-Ray," Benjamin interrupted, "Please listen to what he's saying. That fool bowed up at Sierra before you got here. I thought he was going to attack her."

"The devil is a lie," Sierra chimed in, "I got a two-edge sword that says he wouldn't have gotten away with it without receiving two nubs." She pulled out her switch-blade and laughed, "I'm sorry, Ray-Ray, but you'd be marrying "nubbles" because I would do everything I could to chop his hands off at the wrists. I'm Zorro's twin when it comes to a knife, huntey!"

Benjamin stuck his chest out and beat on it like King Kong and turned to Sierra, "No offense, baby, but you ain't got no punk. Ray-Ray, I'm sorry but you'd be marrying a blind mouse because I will beat his eyeballs out. I'm telling you that my hands are weapons when they need to be." He acted as if he were Muhammed Ali.

"Everyone calm down," Grandma Flo butted in, "Let David finish."

"Thank you, Flo." He picks up the box and pulls out some surveillance equipment. "Now Flo found this hidden camera by accident attached to her light on the front porch. Whoever planted these used top-notch surveillance equipment. I mean, like NSA style. Someone had to pay a pretty penny for it and to have them installed. When she called me and told me something was weird-looking peeking above the light fixture, it prompted me to bring my gear to search. I knew what it was when she pointed it out to me. So, I hunted for more and found another one at the back by a flower pot on the steps. Someone was monitoring who's coming and going at this house."

"Could that be?" I said what I was thinking out loud.

Everyone stared at me. I think we all believed it was Elliot behind it.

Grandma was curious and asked, "Well, what country are you going to David for this lead you're talking about?"

"A source told me a person of interest left the Bahamas and is headed to Rio. If I can find him, then I think he'll fill all the missing pieces to the puzzle.

Ray-Ray, I know you're destined to marry this guy but I need you to stall him to Christmas or next year."

"Um...I get what y'all are saying and trying to do. But I'm not convinced; especially now that I know Daddy didn't kill his parents. What's the motive for him planting surveillance equipment?"

Mr. David shook his head, "I don't know yet, sweetie, that's why I need you to wait."

My phone rang. "Guys it's Mama. Hold on."

CHAPTER 42

DINNER FOR SIX?

James apologizes to Carol for being defensive. "I didn't mean to speak to him that way. I didn't frighten you did I?"

Carol smiled nonchalantly and said, "No. I was a little flattered because it was harmless. I can deal with safe, guiltless jealousy, but I will not tolerate hurtful, destructive jealousy. You'll lose me quick."

James beamed with pride. "Are you saying that 'you're mine'?"

"What?" Carol turned her head as that of an owl.

"Well, you said, '*You'll lose me.*' I take that as you're accepting to be my girl." James grinned with a smile from Earth to Heaven.

She blushed and said, "I guess. I mean, I am fond of you."

They arrived at the restaurant. He got out and opened her door for her.

"By the way, you look very snazzy, love."

"Thank you, James. I like your shirt with those fitting blue jeans."

"Appreciate it. I like to dress casually from time to time."

They enter Ol'Jerry's Seafood, and James kindly says to the hostess, "Dinner for two, please."

As they're seated, Carol is looking around the room and recognizes a familiar face. Immediately, she becomes tense.

"Is everything all right, Carol?" James notices.

"Uh, yeah. I need to go to the restroom. Order me a tea with lemon, please."

She wastes no time for a response from James and darts to the bathroom. Entering the restroom, she looks in the mirror. She feels so much anxiety from seeing Slim that she wishes she could leave. Carol calls Rayna.

"Hello, Mama. Having fun are ya?"

"Ray-Ray, I need you to come get me! Please. I see him."

Rayna's frightened, "Mama, what's wrong!"

"It's Slim! He's here. He said he would kill me if he ever saw me again. I stole his stash of drugs and turned him in to the police so I could get off."

"Where's James? Mama, did that coward leave you by yourself?"

"No, he doesn't know anything about it. I'm in the restroom."

"Look, it's been over 15 years, Mama. Maybe, "Slime," has changed. You are in control now. You got this. Just in case though, I will send Grandma and Mr. David over. Which restaurant?"

"Um, it's Jerry's Seafood. Thanks, baby girl." She hangs up in a panic.

As soon as she hangs up. She says, "Grandma and Mr. David, can you go over to *Ol' Jerry's Seafood*? Mama sees Slim and is worried that he may try something."

"How bout it, David? Will you go with me?"

"Of course, Flo. You know Carol is like a daughter to me."

Benjamin looks confused, "Well, where's my Dad?"

"He's there but Mama doesn't want to involve him."

"Do you need me and Sierra to go too?" He takes Sierra by the hand and looks into her eyes, "You want some shrimp 'n' grits, baby?"

She winks at him, "Sho' 'nuf'! I mean, no offense Grandma Flo, but that appetizer is gone."

I think about it and say, "Well, the more the merrier. Go ahead."

They laugh and head over to the restaurant.

Carol finally comes back to the table and James stands to seat her. "Baby, are you okay? Imma little worried."

"Yeah," she hesitates and looks across the dining room of the restaurant. Slim is glaring at her with some Caucasian woman sitting across from him. James' eyes follow her direction.

"You know him?"

Carol stirs her lemon in the tea with her straw and reluctantly answers, "Um...yeah. He's an ex-boyfriend from my past."

Suddenly, the waitress comes to the table and says, "Your party of four is here. So we're going to move you to a larger table in the party room."

"Excuse me?" James seems annoyed, "Party of four?"

David, Flo, Benjamin, and Sierra surround them with smiles from Earth to Heaven.

"What's going on, guys?" James looks around at them.

"Well, after the refreshments, we were hungry. Sierra suggested shrimp 'n' grits." Benjamin replied.

The waitress returns and leads them to the party room.

Carol could feel Slim's eyes watching her. She glances back and looks in his direction. The woman sitting with him went to the bathroom. Carol reads his lips, "We need to talk."

Carol stops in her tracks. "Excuse me, guys. Go ahead. There's something I need to take care of."

Mr. David takes her by the hand. "Do you need me to come with you?"

"Excuse me, sir," James butted in and takes Carol's other hand, "but I will do that."

"No, neither of you will. I need to do this by myself. I'm not afraid anymore. God is with me and will give me what to say. Now please go on to the table. I will join you shortly."

They agreed to move on and James kissed her gently on the cheek. Carol smiled and blushed.

She walked over to Slim's table. He still looks the same; just a little older. Tall, handsome, slim, and dreadlocks with hints of gray hair. His face and eyes seem calm. Carol gathers her nerves. "Look, I don't want any trouble from you. I've moved on with my life, including rehab, therapy, and a new relationship. Not that any of that is your business. I hope that you can forgive me for..."

"I did a long time ago." Slim said mild-manneredly. I forgave you a long time ago for snitching on me and stealing my stash. You know, those thirteen years in prison opened my eyes, for real. I got sober, got my high school diploma and an associate's degree in Information Technology. I work as a maintenance and repair technician at Sumnerfield Technology Solutions. I wanna thank you. You changed my life."

The woman came back to the table and sat across from him. Slim introduces the woman as his wife and mother of his two teenage sons.

Carol is speechless at first then reaches out to shake both their hands. She tells Slim's wife they were friends long ago and are just catching up. "Congratulations on your future endeavors. I wish you both well." She smiled at both of them and heartily walked to the party room for a dinner of six.

James is about to make an announcement and pulls out a chair for her beside him. He lifts his glass of tea and says, "A toast to each of you for making this such a wonderful evening. I would love it if you would join me for morning worship this Sunday at ten-thirty in Kelton."

Everyone smiles and raises their glass of non-alcoholic beverage and says, "Here, here," including Carol.

CHAPTER 43

TIME TO SPEED THINGS UP

Elliot kept thinking about what Drake said: "*What if they're on to you?*" He might be right, Elliot thought. I have to speed things up. He arrived at Rayna's place and let himself in. He ran around the townhouse removing all the cameras. He placed everything in the trunk of his car. He looked around hoping and praying he hadn't forgotten anything. The ring! He needed to get it back so he could take the chip out.

He heard the key turning in the door and quickly ran to the bathroom, undressed, and hopped in the shower.

"Elliot? Hi, honey. I'm home."

I hear the shower running and begin to smile. I undress and join him to give him his *cookies and cream.* As his hands grazed my wet inner thighs and his masculine hands squeezed the nipples on my tender breasts, I thought, "Oh I wish we could make love like this every day."

"I love you so much, my beautiful," Elliot said repeatedly as we made wild, passionate love.

When we finally landed back on Earth from our '*rocket ride*', Elliot said, "Hey, babe let's get married Monday morning at the Justice of the Peace."

"What's the rush, babe?" I asked apprehensively, "I mean, you haven't even taken care of your affairs about the house in Charlestown."

"You let me worry about all that. I want you to say "I do," beautiful. I can't wait any longer, Rayna. I'm tired of driving back and forth. I wanna be with you...but as your husband. I don't want to...how the old folks put it? Um...*shack up*. So marry me, Rayna. Please."

He leans over, kisses me tenderly on my forehead, and looks into my eyes as though he is looking through the core of my very soul. His soft, kind, beautiful eyes said he truly loved me.

I think to myself as my mind and my heart battle with reason, "I believe and trust God to change this man." Then I tuned out everything loathsome that was spoken or speculated about him. I ignored that still, small voice inside me screaming, "***Noooo***!" And Pastor Nolan's words, "*Pray before you do, dear.*"

I held Elliot's face in my hands and began to shed tears of joy believing I couldn't neglect this man based on some terrible experiences we'd already had. After all, no relationship is perfect, right?

He seemed impatient awaiting my answer and says, "You know what, Rayna? Just forget it." He stood up to get dressed, "If it has to take you that long to answer, then obviously I was mistaken about your feelings for me and what this relationship means to you."

Instantly, I pulled him back to me and held him. "Elliot, I love you. I want you to be my husband. All I need is for us to be on the same page about counseling, trust, and faith in God. Without it, babe, I..."

"Rayna," he laid beside me and held me, "I won't hurt you like that again, baby, I promise. Be my wife and let me prove myself to you."

I sat up and hugged him tightly, "Let's do it! Let's get married Monday morning!"

Elliot smiled eerily as he embraced Rayna, "Thank you, baby, let's surprise everyone after it's done."

"I think that's a great idea! Then I will have two surprises to tell Daddy."

Elliot sat up instantly. "What do you mean, 'two surprises?'"

I forgot about the meeting at Grandma's after being distracted by our lovemaking and Elliot's sudden change in marital plans. "Oh, Mr. David found out that Daddy wasn't responsible for killing your parents in the car accident."

"Come again?" Elliot looked distraught.

"Well, it turns out some man dying of cancer confessed to switching Daddy to the driver's seat before he fled the scene of the accident."

"That can't be! The paper said your Daddy was arrested, tried, and sent to prison for about 10 years."

"Wrongly convicted based on Jason Turner's confession," I reminded him, "And when I tell Daddy, I'm sure the State is going to have to compensate. Tasha will insist."

"This Mr. David. Is he the same man that found your Dad?"

"Yeah. He's a former detective turned private eye and my Grandpa Harry's best friend."

Then Elliot's mind recalled, "*The ring*!" He glanced around the room and saw it on the nightstand. He assumed she must have taken it off before getting in the shower.

"Um, Queen," he hugged her while eyeing the ring, "I'm thirsty. Will you get me a glass of wine, please?"

"Gladly, my King," she laughs as she scampers nakedly to the kitchen. But not without picking up the ruby ring first and putting it on.

Elliot panics. "I have to get that ring back." His face is tight and his fists are clenched. He's about to punch the wall but halts. He remembered, "I must control it. That private eye may be on to me." Overcome with anger, he punches the pillows on the bed instead.

Chapter 44

House of Prayer MBC

Why is my phone ringing so early? Oh, it's Mama.

"Hi, Mama. You okay?"

"Yeah, Slim said he forgives me and was glad I snitched on him. Girl, he married and got two boys."

"Mama, I love you, but it's 6:30 in the morning. Can I call you later?"

"Well, I was calling because we're leaving to go to James' church in a couple of hours. I wanted to see if you're going?"

"I'm sorry, but no. Y'all drive safe. Pray for me. Love you."

"Love you too."

Carol took a shower and tried to figure out what she was going to wear. In the end, she decided on a black bell-bottom pantsuit accented with a canary sleeveless blouse and a black and white necklace for her outfit.

When she got downstairs, Mr. David arrived looking dapper as ever wearing a navy Armani suit with a pink shirt and blue and pink pinstriped tie. He was holding a navy wide-brim fedora in his hand.

"Good morning, Mr. David. Don't you look handsome?"

He stands to hug Carol and kiss her on the cheek, "Thank you, dear."

"Watch out, you're going have to fight 'em off this morning."

Grandma comes from the kitchen wearing a pink and navy floral dress with a matching pink hat. "Fight who off? Girl, they betta step aside."

"What?" Carol smiled. "Since when Mama?"

"Chile, mind your business. We grown."

"Oh, you get no objection here. I think it's great!" She gives them both a hug.

"All right ladies. We better get a move on."

Mr. David stands to open the door for them.

"Yeah," Grandma Flo twisted her hat to the side and said, "Sierra called me and said she and Benjamin are going to meet us there."

The Browns Get Ready

"Guys come on! It's time to get up. We don't want to be late," Aunt Hilda Mae yelled from the kitchen. She fixed a big breakfast with biscuits, bacon, grits, eggs, and pancakes.

Everyone came rushing in.

"Slow down kids," Tasha was trying to fix their plate.

"It smells great, Mommy." Latisha turned to Aunt Hilda Mae and said, "Thank you, Grandma!"

"Yeah, thanks Grandma," Anthony echoed.

Aunt Hilda Mae began to cry. Raymond walked over to console her. "Well, you did help raise me. You're entitled."

The twins gave her a hug and everyone sat down to eat.

"Let us pray," Raymond said. Tasha and the kids looked at him surprisingly and smiled at him. They ate and scurried around to get dressed.

A quick family photo was taken in the living room as everyone wore matching shades of mint green and black.

Except, the bright yellow and navy blue floral dress that Aunt Hilda Mae wore, along with her yellow hat and navy shoes, made her stand out.

Chapter 45

CHURCH TIME

Benjamin and Sierra were getting out of the car as Mama, Mr. David, and Grandma pulled up at the House of Prayer Missionary Baptist Church. They greeted each other and went inside.

The ushers welcomed them in as the choir was singing "Pass Me Not, O' Gentle Savior." James was delighted when he saw Carol and his son. He motioned for one of the ushers to seat them up front. The congregation's eyes followed as they walked by.

Aunt Hilda Mae waved to Grandma Flo.

Raymond was smitten when he saw Carol. Without thinking, he calmly and quietly said, "Carol?"

Tasha looked at him sharply and said, "Oh yeah, Raymond? We'll talk after service."

Aunt Hilda Mae leaned over the twins and whispered to Raymond, "Boy, Carol looks good, doesn't she?"

Raymond didn't say a word and just looked at the floor as the choir finished the hymnal.

James was overjoyed and announced, "Well, saints and friends, I'm pleased to see some special visitors with us today. I'm going to ask this exceptional woman of God and dear lady to please stand." He looked at her with gleaming eyes and said, "Sister Carol Jennings."

Everyone clapped when she stood up and the murmurings began. Tasha seems relieved as she realizes that Pastor Nolan is in love with Carol. She glances over at Raymond whose jaw is clenched tight.

"I would also like for my son, Benjamin, and his significant other, Sierra, to stand."

Now the congregants appear confused that he has a son, but they clap anyhow.

He replied, "My topic for today is "*Confession is Good for the Soul*." Pastor Nolan goes on to explain how confessing your faults to God releases the guilt from your soul. Then he tells the congregation about how he had to go away to get help in order to lead by example. He let them know he wasn't ashamed to go to rehab and recovery or seek counsel. "Saints and friends, I was having a mental breakdown after suffering the loss of my family. I had to turn to God for an answer because I was struggling with continuing to be a Pastor and a Christian. I didn't even know if I wanted to live anymore. Depression had taken over my soul, my mind, and my heart. How many know that God is a God of a second chance and HE will deliver you?"

Many raised both hands while others shouted, "Amen, Pastor."

Pastor Nolan began to shed tears. "You know, I am not a perfect man, but I know God has restored my faith, my joy, and my peace. He sent me to that rehab and recovery center in Sumnerfield which is how I met the lovely 'Carol'." He looks at her and smiles as he wipes away his tears, and she gives him a warm smile.

"To my wonderful son who stood by my side every step of the way, I appreciate you. You mean the world to me. I tell you saints and friends when I was young I fathered a son that I was unaware of. But God knew I would need this young man in my life. God is restoring my life and I owe HIM everything." Pastor Nolan looks at Benjamin, who is crying and Sierra is wiping his tears with a handkerchief,

"Saints and friends, confess your faults to the Lord. Be released from your guilt and regret today. If you desire prayer, please come to the altar."

Benjamin, Sierra, and Carol stood to go to the altar.

Raymond, Tasha, and the twins came too. Carol glanced at Raymond and smiled. Tasha glared at Raymond, dug her fingernails deep into his hand, and whispered, "We'll talk after service." Raymond's hand was in pain as her sharp nails felt like pins sticking in him. He managed to say, "It's okay, Tasha."

Pastor Nolan gave the prayer and the benediction. He could hardly wait to talk to Carol. And Raymond couldn't either.

Aunt Hilda Mae and Grandma Flo started catching up. Aunt Hilda Mae shared that she has a doctor's appointment on Tuesday and that she suspects she'll be moving to Kelton with Raymond and Tasha.

"I think that's wonderful Hilda Mae. We'll have to get together before you leave Sumnerfield. I can also come up to visit you in Kelton sometime and we can go out to eat."

"That's fine, Florence. But now there's a Deacon been eyeing me and I might want to get acquainted. I see you and David are hanging out. Is it serious yet?"

"No, not yet. I do enjoy spending time with him. I guess because he reminds me of Harry."

"You have to let Harold go, Florence. I think David's a good guy. Give him a chance. Harold would approve."

"I know you're right. But I don't think I'm ready."

They both hug each other and Aunt Hilda Mae promises to call Florence after the doctor's visit.

Carol gets ready to stroll over to James when Raymond grabs her by the hand. "Hi, Carol. You look great!"

"Thanks, Raymond. You look nice as well. So, is that Mrs. Brown, I saw?"

"It sure is," Tasha comes from out of nowhere with the twins.

"Mommy, I'm ready to go," Latisha whined.

"Daddy, I'm hungry," Anthony tugged Raymond's coat.

"Okay, guys we're getting ready to go. But first, I want you to meet Ray Ray's mother. This is Ms. Carol."

They both tell her hello and run over to Aunt Hilda Mae.

"Hey babe, I want you to meet Carol." Raymond appears nervous.

Tasha reaches to shake Carol's hand. "How are you, Carol?"

"I'm doing fine. I came to be with James...I mean, Pastor Nolan. He invited me."

"Are y'all dating?" Tasha asked nosily.

"Tasha!" Raymond sounded annoyed.

"Oh, it's okay. We are interested in each other but just taking it slow."

James comes over and kisses Carol gently on the cheek. Raymond's face tightens.

Carol introduced them and Tasha had a smile from Earth to Heaven. She realized it was not Carol she was worried about but noticed her husband was having difficulty grappling with Carol's and Pastor Nolan's relationship.

James slips his arm around Carol's waist. "Well, dear, would you like to go to lunch?"

"Sure," Carol said shyly and leaned on him.

Raymond jumps in, "Where'd you plan on going? Maybe Tasha and I could join you."

"Well," Tasha interrupted, "We can't Raymond because Aunt Hilda Mae is cooking for us. I think it would be rude to disappoint her. And besides, let the Pastor and Carol enjoy their moment alone."

"Thank you, Sister Tasha," James chimed in, "I **would** like to discuss some things with Carol. No offense, but maybe another time, Brother Raymond."

Inside, Raymond's blood was boiling with jealousy. He shook James' hand and walked away without saying anything to Carol. Tasha shook both their hands and said, "Goodbye. Enjoy your lunch."

CHAPTER 46

SUNDAY DINNER PROPOSAL

Everyone said their goodbyes and headed back to Sumnerfield; except Carol. James agreed to take her home that evening after lunch and possibly dinner.

They decided to eat at *Red's Que Shack* at the Kelton Mall. Carol wore a radiant smile as James seated her at the table.

Leaning in, he said, "Why are you smiling so hard, Queen?"

Carol gleamed like a shy schoolgirl, "I'm truly enjoying this day. Your sermon was so inspiring and moving. I'm proud of you for sharing your confession and pain with your congregation. The way I see it, transparency shows how much you care about and respect them. It speaks volumes of your character."

"Well, God is real with us and I want to be real with the people. That's why it was so important to get help and share my testimony. I also want to be real with you, Carol."

She looks into his eyes as he grabs her by the hand and gets down on one knee beside her. "Man, what are you doing?" Carol appears to be embarrassed and notices people are staring.

"Woman, just go with the flow," he says as he reaches into his pocket and pulls out a small, black velvet box. "Look, I've only known you a short time but know that I want to spend a lifetime with you." And he starts to sing Joe Cocker's *"You Are So Beautiful"* as everyone in the restaurant looks on in awe. When he finishes serenading her, Carol immediately hugs him and says, "Yes!" as he slips the diamond ring on her finger. "Oh my goodness! I can't believe it." She kisses him softly on the lips. He begins to cry.

Everyone gave a standing ovation and shouted, "Congratulations!"

"You've made me so happy, Carol. I thought my life was over. I'm so glad I found you." Looking towards Heaven while caressing her small frame, he whispers,

" Thank you, God."

Carol hugged him and whispered, "Amen, Pastor! Were you planning this all weekend?"

"No, I had the ring in the glove compartment and, I was planning to wait until Christmas. But, after seeing your angelic face in the crowd today confirmed what I needed to do. You and I are going to be a testimony to many people, Carol."

"I can't wait to tell, Mama and Ray-Ray! Do you mind if we have a church wedding? Here, in Kelton?"

"Of course not. Whatever you want. You plan it and go all out if you want to. Let me know the finances, okay?"

"Okay. How soon are we talking?"

"Whenever you want, baby. I just pray it's not five or ten years from now." They both laugh.

"It won't be that long, trust me. I'm thinking Christmas Eve?"

"Sure, why not? Let's do it," James said with excitement.

"Ray-Ray's getting married on Thanksgiving Day and us on Christmas Eve! God is good!"

"Yes, *HE* is," James reiterates, "Now, I have a question."

"What's that, sweetie?" She says while gazing at her ring.

"Are we going to have trouble outta Brother Raymond?"

"No!" Carol turns and looks at him. "Why do you ask that?"

"I don't believe he thought kindly of the way I was holding you by the waist. I saw his clenched jaw."

"But he's married with children. And besides, we were over since Ray-Ray was about five or six."

"You know that, but I don't think he believes it."

"Well, I'm with whom God has given me. I love you, James Nolan."

CHAPTER 47

SUNDAY DINNER SPAT

As soon as Raymond and Tasha got in the car after church service, Tasha said heatedly, "Raymond, what's up with you? Do you have any unfinished business with Carol you want me to know about?"

Raymond began rubbing his head feeling anxiety coming on. With a saddened, gloomy look as though he just found out about the death of a loved one, he calmly said, "Not now, Tasha. Not in front of the kids. We'll talk later."

"You bet we will," she said as she snatched her seatbelt and put it on.

"Look you two," Aunt Hilda Mae noticed the tension between them, "Get it together. Don't let the past block your future. You both need to let it go; especially **you**, Raymond. Now I mean it. Carol has moved on and, you should've accepted that before you married Tasha."

Raymond respectfully declined to say anything and drove home. The twins were too busy playing *'rock, paper, scissors'*, they were not aware of anything wrong.

Everyone changed clothes and Aunt Hilda Mae began cooking meatloaf, homemade mashed potatoes, collard greens, cornbread muffins, and a banana pudding for dessert. Tasha went in to help but she pushed her out of the kitchen.

"I work alone, chile."

"But, I just want to help Aunt Hilda Mae."

"Thank you, but no. Go relax. Talk to your husband."

The twins ran to play outside in the fenced backyard and Raymond sat on the patio to watch them. Tasha peered through the window and saw he looked as though he were in deep thought and miles from home.

She walked away with tears in her eyes, went to the bathroom, and prayed, "Lord, I need you to help me with my emotions about my husband's love for Carol. I don't feel it's her fault, God. I don't even think she noticed how he still feels about her. But I need you, Lord, to take away this jealousy and rage I feel inside towards Raymond. I'm trying to be understanding. Help me, Lord. I don't want to lose my husband. Please give me the words to say. Speak Lord and I shall obey. In Jesus' name. Amen."

"All right, everyone. Dinner's ready. Wash up, please," Aunt Hilda Mae yelled from the kitchen.

Everyone sat down to eat except Raymond. Aunt Hilda Mae glanced at Tasha and could tell she had been crying.

Aunt Hilda Mae hugged her, "Tasha, it's okay. Everything will work out. He loves you. It's just he hasn't seen Carol since they split up and it flooded his mind with memories of how things were."

"You don't have to make excuses for him," Tasha said angrily and pushed her away, "He's a grown man with a decision he needs to make."

"Who are you raising your voice at, chile? You betta talk to me with respect. Now I'm not making excuses for him. I'm telling you how it is. Don't give that man an ultimatum or you'll lose him. Talk to him about how it's making you feel."

"Oh, I am. You can believe that. I saw how he was sitting on the patio thinking about her. He probably wants to leave me and the kids for her."

"Calm down, Tasha, and stop overreacting." Aunt Hilda Mae advised her.

Tasha slams her fork down on the table, "Overreacting! Are you kidding me, Aunt Hilda Mae? My husband is not eating dinner with us right now because he's on the patio reminiscing about another woman and you're telling *me* to 'stop overreacting'!"

The children looked at Tasha confused and nervous,

"Mommy, what's wrong?" Anthony asked.

"Are you and Daddy fighting, Mommy?" Latisha started crying.

"No, Tisha," Anthony said, "Grandma and Mommy are fighting."

Aunt Hilda Mae ran over and hugged the twins. "Everything's okay, babies, sometimes grownups have disagreements just like children."

Tasha runs to the bedroom and slams the door.

Raymond is coming out of the bathroom and it appears he has been crying. He sits on the bed beside Tasha and holds her hands. "Look, baby, I'm sorry I upset you. I won't lie to you, Tasha. Seeing Carol today, brought up some emotions in me from years ago. I was only a little jealous because I saw how much she had changed and I thought it should've been with me. I do have feelings for her, and possibly even still love her. But not like you think though. She's the mother of my daughter and I will always cherish that because I wouldn't have Ray-Ray if it weren't for her.

I don't regret anything Carol and I had together. It doesn't replace what I have now. When you came into my life, baby, you saved me from my past. God gave us each other; to be here for one another. I love you, baby. Please believe that. It's you I want."

He hugs her and gently kisses her tears. They lock the bedroom door after putting out the 'Do Not Disturb' sign.

CHAPTER 48

STORMY WEDDING DAY

I awakened to thunder and lightning that Monday morning. I think God was warning me not to marry Elliot today. I turned the TV on and the weather alert told of flash floods, heavy rain, and wind gusts up to 40 mph.

I looked over at Elliot and he was fast asleep. I got up and showered and went into the kitchen to make breakfast. When I opened the blinds, I saw my flower pot sailing across the yard. I ran to the bedroom and woke Elliot up. "Baby, get up. It's like a tornado outside or something. Look at the news."

Elliot rubbed his eyes and yawned. He got up and slowly walked to the bathroom. "What's all that noise outside, babe?"

"That's what I'm trying to tell you. The news said there's a flash flood warning and wind gusts up to 40 mph."

"Oh, that's not too bad. We can still make it to the Justice of the Peace."

"Um, baby...I want us to get married but___"

Elliot sounds angry, "But what, Rayna? This is just a sign that nothing can stop us. Life is about taking risks. Stop your whining and get dressed. We need to be there at 10:00." Elliot looked out the bedroom window and saw debris floating on the flooded streets and tree limbs falling in the park.

All of sudden the lights flickered. Rayna replied, "Baby, do you think God is trying to tell us to wait?"

"Don't start Rayna. Get dressed." Angrily, he raised his hand in the air.

I flinched trying to smile past the fear. "Aren't you hungry? I was going to make breakfast."

He grabbed me by the waist and kissed me on the neck. "Look, we'll have plenty of time for food later. C'mon, shower with me."

"But I just took a shower."

"Now, please," he said. And pulled me into the shower with him and made love to me like some wild beast.

"Elliot, baby, you're hurting me."

"I need you, Rayna!" He pushed harder while squeezing my neck and biting my breasts.

It was as though he didn't hear me. He kept going until he was satisfied.

Afterward, I was crying as I got dressed.

"What's wrong with you now?"

"Elliot, you hurt me. I don't like rough sex."

"Ah, I'm sorry, baby. You make me crazy like that." He kissed her gently on the lips. "Now go on and get dressed."

I was sore and noticed a few bruises on my thighs. I put on the white dress he bought me and he put on a black Armani suit with a white shirt and black tie.

"Ray-Ray, here are the rings." He showed them to me with a smile from Earth to Heaven. For the first time, I saw a genuine smile that made his eyes gleam with excitement.

I held him by the hand and looked into his eyes. "You do love me, don't you?"

He kissed my forehead and said, "Of course, I do, silly; especially, now that I know your Daddy didn't kill my parents. Because I was gonna have to kill him."

"Seriously, Elliot? That's not funny baby."

He rushed to her side and kissed her on the small of her neck. "I won't hurt you, Ray-Ray. I love you, girl!

I looked out the window and the rain seemed to be drizzling now with no sun in sight. The winds had calmed down. Debris was everywhere. The town trucks were out cleaning up.

"Well, Rayna, just think, when we return, you will be Mrs. Elliot Nolan."

"I know," as I smiled as that small, faint voice popped in my head, "Pray before you do, dear."

We ran to the car and jumped in. He didn't even open the door for me. I guess that was okay. After all, it was raining.

When we got to the Justice of the Peace, there were two couples ahead of us...the soon-to-be Dawsons and Schwartz'. Elliot was excited and held my hand tightly.

"Are you okay, Elliot?"

"Yeah, why do you ask?"

"My hand...you're squeezing my hand."

He looked down at her hand and saw he was leaving a mark. He quickly let go and apologized. "I guess I'm not okay, baby. I'm nervous. I want to be a good husband to you like my dad was to my mom. I don't want to lose you, Rayna. I didn't mean to hurt your hand."

"Baby, don't you think we should wait," Rayna asked again.

"No, I'll be okay once we get married. I'm no good when I'm overly anxious."

"I see." I convince him to let's wait in the hallway. So he can pace his anxiety away.

We see the Dawson's go in and Elliot becomes more nervous. I rub his back to calm him. "Elliot, we need witnesses."

"Yeah, right. Can you ask that couple in there?"

I asked the soon-to-be Schwartz' if they'd be our witnesses and they happily accepted. I saw Elliot sweating profusely. "Baby, you've got to calm down. You look like you're about to faint. I'll get you some water." I quickly find a vending machine and get him a bottle of water. I stop by the bathroom and wet some paper towels. When I return, Elliot has his head down. "Elliot, what's wrong? Here, drink this water."

He drinks it quickly as though he were in a desert. I put the wet towels on his forehead. He breathes in and out slowly. He starts to calm down. The Schwartzes came out to let us know they were ready for us. And just like that...we did it!

CHAPTER 49

AUNT HILDA MAE'S DOCTOR VISIT

Aunt Hilda Mae was nervous when they arrived at her doctor's appointment. "I don't know why they have to do all these tests at one time," she complained.

Tasha reassured her, "It's going to be all right. It's procedure given your age. I mean, you are sixty- seven now."

"So. What's age got to do with it? I'll be glad when it's over."

Raymond decided to stay with the twins in Kelton. He said he was tired and didn't feel like going.

A nurse came to the waiting area and called, "Ms. Hilda Mae Leake?"

Aunt Hilda Mae stood up and followed her to the patient room while Tasha sat and waited.

Tasha walked over to get a magazine off the rack and noticed a middle-aged lady sitting in a corner nearby. Thinking to herself, "It looks like her. Nah, it can't be."

She was getting ready to walk away when the lady said, "Hi. Sister Tasha?"

"Excuse me? Do I know you?" Tasha seemed defensive.

"Not really. We met briefly at church on Sunday. I'm Carol."

"Oh, you're Ray-Ray's mother." Then Tasha notices the engagement ring on her finger. "I see your lunch date with Pastor Nolan was wonderful."

Carol was startled, "Excuse me?"

Tasha points to the ring.

"Um, yes. It was." she beamed with excitement.

"I recognize that smile from Earth to Heaven anywhere, love bird."

"Sister Tasha, he makes me feel so special and like..."

"Like you're the only one," Tasha butted in.

"Yes!" Carol exclaimed. "Our connection seems as though we've known each other all our lives. I don't have to pretend with him, and, I've never been nervous around him. He has such a good heart."

"Sounds like you're madly in love with him."

"Oh, I am."

Another nurse came out and yelled, "Carol Jennings?"

Carol quickly waved to her and told Tasha she was pleased to see her again before she was escorted to a patient room.

Tasha thinks about how Raymond might respond when she tells him that his once true love is getting hitched. She picked up her phone and was about to call him when a nurse tapped her shoulder and asked her to come to Aunt Hilda Mae's room.

When they arrived at the room, Aunt Hilda Mae was crying and the doctor was sitting on a rolling stool near her. Tasha hugged her and said, "What's wrong?"

The doctor introduced himself as "Doctor Howard Cash" and explained that Aunt Hilda Mae was showing signs of dementia and he wanted to put her on medication but she refused. "I understand that you're a nurse, right?"

"I am," Tasha replied.

"Well, I was hoping you would talk it over with her about how beneficial it will be if she starts the medications."

"I don't want it, Tasha," Aunt Hilda Mae cried, "I'm already taking blood pressure and diabetes pills. I think they trying to kill me."

"Aunt Hilda Mae that's simply not true. These pills will help you feel better. Remember, you want to be here for the twins. You want to be able to cook for them and read to them, right?"

"Of course, I do. They need some meat on their bones."

Dr. Cash chuckled, "So does this mean you will try the medication, Ms. Leake?"

"I reckon so." She protested.

Tasha hugged her. "Thank you, Dr. Cash." They checked out and were on their way to the car.

"Hey, Ms. Hilda Mae," Carol called out from across the parking lot.

Aunt Hilda Mae ran to greet her, "Oh my goodness, Carol! You look so wonderful. I'm proud of you, baby."

"Thank you so much."

"Girl, you got a smile from Earth to Glory! What are you beaming for?"

Carol flashed the diamond in front of her face. "Lord have mercy, chile. Tasha, that ring bigger than yours ain't it?" Aunt Hilda Mae said looking back at her.

Carol blushed, "Ms. Hilda Mae you are still a mess! James and I hope you all can come to the wedding at 11:00 on Christmas Eve at *House of Prayer*."

"I'll let **my** husband know, Tasha replied sarcastically, "Congratulations, *Mrs. Nolan*!"

"Thank you. Y'all take care," Carol ignored Tasha's sarcasm as she hugged Aunt Hilda Mae again.

Chapter 50

Rayna's Announcement

"I can't believe we're married, babe!" Elliot said excitedly as they started packing for their seven-day honeymoon in the Bahamas.

"I know, right?" I hugged him as I got out of the shower.

He kissed me over and over again. Then he began to cry. "I wish my parents and my brother were here to see this."

I held him close to me and rocked him in my arms. He finally pulled himself together. I quickly got dressed before calling Mama and Grandma. Mama had called me several times and I wasn't able to talk to her.

"Hi, Mama. I see you called me several times yesterday and, I want to apologize. Is everything okay?"

"Yes!" Carol started laughing.

I can hear Grandma in the background, "Have you told her yet?"

"Told me what, Mama?"

"Well, James and I are getting married on Christmas Eve at 11:00 and I want you to be my maid of honor."

"Oh my goodness, Mama! That's wonderful! I'm so happy for you. But I can't be your maid of honor."

"And why not?" Mama was upset.

"Well, Mama and Grandma...Elliot and I got married yesterday! So I guess that will make me your matron of honor."

Mama and Grandma were both silent.

I felt my heart drop...then ache. I began to cry.

Elliot grabbed the phone from me. "Hi, Ms. Carol. I understand your disappointment in me but, I wish you could at least be happy for Rayna. I'm going to do right by her. You'll see. In a couple of hours, we're leaving for the Bahamas for our honeymoon."

Carol was speechless. Grandma grabbed the phone from her. "Listen, Elliot, she knows we love her and will have to respect her decision. It's just that your behavior hasn't proven to us that you love her."

"But I do love her, Ms. Florence. I will prove it. I promise. I need y'all to give me a chance."

Carol motioned for her to give back the phone. "Look, if you can't use your hands except to hug or bathe my daughter, then I suggest you get an annulment now because nothing will stop me from laying hands on you or even...Just because I know Jesus doesn't mean I don't remember the streets. You get my drift."

"Yes ma'am. Here's Rayna." He hands the phone back to her.

"Hey, Mama."

"Hey, baby girl. I'm sorry. If you're happy, Ray-Ray, then I'm happy for you. I just want you to be safe."

"I know, Mama, but I'm a lady now...not a little girl."

"Ray-Ray, you'll always be my little girl."

"I understand that but the mistakes I make in life are mine. I married Elliot because I believe he does love me. I want to give my husband a chance."

"Okay, baby. Put your phone on speaker. Can you both hear me?"

They both say, "Yes ma'am."

"Look, I want to apologize to both of you. Elliot, welcome to the family, son. God bless you. I love you. Please be safe in the Bahamas."

"Thank you, Ms. Jennings, Elliot replied. "Thank you, Mama. We'll call as soon as we land."

I felt so much better now.

Elliot hugged me and said, "She called me *'son'*. Did you hear that, Rayna?"

"I heard her, baby. Mama is sweet like that. Oh, Mr. Nolan, I love you."

"I love you more, Mrs. Nolan."

"Speaking of which, baby, Mama is going to be Mrs. Nolan too!"

"Excuse me?"

"Yep. She and Pastor Nolan are getting married on Christmas Eve. Isn't that wonderful!"

Elliot's face tightens and he goes to the bathroom and quietly closes the door. He's about to punch the mirror.

"Baby, are you okay in there?"

He stares angrily into the mirror and takes a deep breath, "Yeah, I'm good." He turns on the faucet and sees the ruby ring. He smiles and breathes a sigh of
relief before he slips it into his pocket.

"So, your mom is going to be my mother-in-law and auntie, huh?"

"It looks like it. Let's go, babe. Bahamas! Here comes the Nolans!"

Elliot begins to load the car. I run to the door and ask, "Baby, I can't find my ring. Did you see it in the bathroom?"

"Nah, babe. It's okay. I'll buy you a new one."
"You're not upset with me?"
"No. it's no big deal. I got you!"
I closed the door behind me and gave him the biggest hug.

CHAPTER 51

MR. DAVID'S UPDATE

When Carol hangs up the phone with Ray-Ray, she overhears Florence talking to Mr. David. Florence has a worried look on her face.

"You say you're in Rio, David?"

"Yeah, Florence. My informant told me that my lead high-tailed it out of the Bahamas. He's some guy that went to school with Elijah, Elliot's brother."

"Do you know the lead's name?" "Well, I have a friend who's a former FBI agent, and he pulled some strings to trace the surveillance equipment. The person of interest's name is Drake Hudson."

"Be careful, David," Florence says concernedly, "Oh! I have some good news and bad news."

"What is it, Florence?"

"Um, Ray-Ray already married Elliot. That's the bad news."

"What?" David was angry. "I told her to wait until I finished my investigation. Elliot could be dangerous. Especially, if he killed those people."

"We know but somehow he convinced her and they went ahead. David, I'm worried because he's taking her to the Bahamas on their honeymoon."

"You and Carol don't worry. I have a couple of friends there. I'll put a tail on them. You said you had some good news too?"

"Yeah, Carol and James are getting married on Christmas Eve and she wants you to give her away."

"Oh, man. That's awesome! You know I'd be glad to do it. I sure wish Harry was here." David's phone beeped. "Florence, my informant is beeping in. I'll call you later."

"Okay. Thank you, David."

CHAPTER 52

BAHAMA DRAMA

We're finally here! An enchanting paradise with soft, white sand, turquoise blue waters, and clear, blue skies, Atlantis is one of the most alluring places in the world! I can't wait to get to our private cabana at The Coral!

"Babe, I need a drink," I told Elliot.

"Okay, let's get settled in first and then go down to the bar."

We quickly put our things in our cabana. I ordered a margarita and Elliot got a gin and tonic. He drank his straight away and said, "Babe, I need to check on something. I will be right back."

I am confused because what newlywed is going to leave his spouse at the bar? Alone. In another country around strangers.

I quickly snap at him. "I'll just go back to the room and wait for you there. I don't want to sit here around *these* people without you."

"Stop your whining! Sit here until I get back!"

"Where are you going? What is so important that you have to leave me sitting here by myself, baby?"

"Look, woman!" He clenches his fist and slams it on the bar. People begin to stare and, I begin to feel embarrassed. I try to hug him but, he pushes me away and walks off.

I sit in disbelief. Suddenly, a man comes over to me and says, "Are you okay, Miss?"

"I'm fine. Please leave me alone."

"I just want to...He reaches into his pocket and hands her a card that says: Richard Lakes, Private Eye Services, LLC.

"Who are you? Why are you giving this to me?" I feel scared now and get ready to go to the room.

"Hey, wait! I need to talk to you. You may be in danger." He grabs me by my arm.

"Stop!" I snatch away from him and run to the room. I lock the door and begin to cry. I notice my hands are shaking. "Where is Elliot?" I think to myself.

Suddenly, there's a knock at the door. "Miss, I need to talk to you about the man you're with. Please let me in. Your grandfather, David, sent me down here to look out for you. That man you're with is dangerous."

"Go away and leave me alone, *please*!"

"Hey! Get away from there.! Who are you?"

Thank God it's Elliot! I run to the door and fling it open! A fight ensues and Elliot is punching and kicking the man repeatedly.

I start yelling at Elliot, "Stop, baby, you're going to kill him!"

Elliot finally does let go and the man limps away with bloody clothes and a bloody face. I prayed he would be okay and wouldn't press charges. I look at Elliot and he's gazing wild-eyed at me. He pushed me into the room and slapped me to the floor. "Who was that? Your boyfriend? Are you cheating on me already? I was only gone about 15 minutes. Get up, heifer!"

"Elliot, please! I didn't do anything wrong. He said he thought I was in danger."

"**Danger**? What are you talking about?"

"He's a private eye."

"What! A private eye?" Elliot is nervous now. "Tell me exactly what he said!" He grabs me and throws me on the couch.

I fear for my life now. "Elliot, what's going on? I want to go home. I'm scared."

"Ho, what did he say?" He yelled and slapped me again.

I felt as though I was going to pass out. I tried to catch my breath to talk. "This man came up to me and gave me a card saying that he's a private eye and that my life may be in danger because of you. What's going on? I don't understand why he would tell me that. Where were you?"

"Let's pack up. Get some rest. We're leaving for Rio tomorrow."

"Elliot, I don't want to go to Rio. I don't even want to be here anymore. I want to go home!"

"Well, you're not. We're going to Rio. Go take a shower and clean yourself up."

"I want an annulment, Elliot. You haven't changed at all. I'm sick of this."

"Look, baby. You are not leaving me. You can't. You love me and you know it. You wanna know where I was?"

"I don't care anymore."

He reaches into his pocket and pulls out a little red velvet box.

I knock it out of his hand, and I storm off to the bathroom and lock the door. "It's not going to work, Elliot. I don't care about your **'*beat-down*'** gifts. If this is the only way I can receive gifts from you, then you can keep 'em! I don't want anything from you!"

There was complete silence. I waited to see if he would come knocking on the door. But nothing. I waited some more. Still nothing. I yelled out, "Elliot, do you hear me?" Complete silence. No answer.

I slowly open the door. It's quiet. I look around the room. He's gone! I look in the corner. His bags are gone! There's the red velvet box, $2,000, and a note on the table that read:

"GO HOME! I will explain when I get back from Rio. Despite how you feel about me or what you think, Rayna, I love you and I'm crazy about you. I will never let you go!"

CHAPTER 53

THE CHASE IN RIO

"Hello?" I'm sorry I can't talk right now, Flo. We're hot on the tail of Drake. He spotted our tail and hauled butt. What's wrong?"

"Ray-Ray just called me and screaming and crying that Elliot beat up one of your men in the Bahamas. That man in the hospital, David! I'm worried about Ray and you. Elliot's on his way to Rio."

"What? Well, is Ray-Ray with him?"

"No, he smacked her around and she on her way back here."

"Good! Get her to your house, Flo, and keep her there. She's in danger! I gotta go. We got Drake surrounded!" He hung up.

Drake sat in the car with several police cars swarming around him like angry, famished sharks. He grabbed the steering wheel tightly. He wondered if he should try to make a break for it and go out with a bang. Then he thought, "If I give myself up and testify against Elliot, then they may give me a lighter sentence. He stares at the flashing, blue lights and holds his hands straight up in the air.

The police come over with guns drawn, yank him out of the car, and throw him to the ground. An officer reads him his rights and cuffs him. David walked up to Drake and said, "Elliot is on his way here for you. We suspect he's coming to kill you. You may be in danger. You better cooperate with these guys if you know what's good for you."

"Oh, I plan to sing for a deal. Don't worry. How y'all gettin' me back to the States?"

"Everything is already taken care of. You just make sure you serenade them when you get back to North Carolina. Boy, am I glad we got to you first."

They both look up as another gentleman is walking towards them with papers in his hand. He takes Drake from the police officer and gives the officer the papers.

"Who are you?" Drake sounded nervous.

The man flashes his badge to David and Drake. "Excuse me. F.B.I. Agent Johnson. Drake before we take you back to the States, we are going to ask you for a favor."

"Scratch my back first. What's up?"

"We know that you're involved in the murders with Elliot Nolan."

"Hey, wait a minute, man. I ain't did no murders. I just set up surveillance cameras for him. I told Elliot that I wouldn't do all that. Look, what do you have in mind, man? Otherwise, I'm going to lawyer up before y'all try to pin murders on me."

"Well, we know Elliot is on the way here looking for you. So, we want you to oblige him."

"Man, that fool crazy! He already threatened me which is why I left the Bahamas!"

"All we need for you to do is call him and let him know that you need some more cash or you're going to start talking. Tell him to meet you at the airport so you can grab a flight to Buenos Aires. We'll be right there with you. We will need you to wear a wire as well."

"I don't know, man...I mean, Elliot is kinda weird. He always edgy about something. He ain't like Elijah was...his brother."

David butted in. "Listen Drake. I wish you would reconsider because my god-granddaughter's life is in danger too. Elliot married her, and I think he's going to try to kill her once he gets back to the States. He's spiraling out of control. He knows we are closing in. Please help them catch him."

"Excuse me, sir, but who are you?" Agent Johnson asked.

"I'm a retired detective turned private eye. I've been working on a case for a close acquaintance of mine. Elliot's wife's grandmother. I have been digging into his past which led me to Drake."

"Hey hold up," Agent Johnson thought. "Let's rethink this. We all know how smart Elliot is. Now he may not go for Drake's excuse to meet him. So, what if we."

"The devil is a lie! Not my Ray-Ray! You will not use her as bait. Figure out a better way to use Drake!"

"Sir, please hear me out. We will have her surrounded. And Drake too!"

"Nah, I ain't being nobody's bait! I will testify against him and that's it."

"All right. Let's discuss this further in the States."

CHAPTER 54

WHAT DO I DO?

"Grandma, what are you doing here?"

"Oh my goodness! Your face, Ray-Ray. I'm calling the police!"

"Oh no, you're not! Please leave, Grandma!"

"I certainly will not. David said for you to come stay with me until they catch Elliot."

"Grandma y'all need to stay outta my personal life."

"If you don't take heed chile, you ain't gone have a life. Personal or otherwise. He's going to kill you Ray if you stay in this toxic mess."

"Well, Granddaddy didn't *kill* you. He hit you too, right? Elliot loves me. He's suffered a lot. Y'all just don't understand him."

"Understand him? Girl, he killed at least three of his family members."

"What are you talking about?"

"Please come home with me and wait for David to get back. He will explain it all. He said you **have** to come and stay with me. Your life is in danger."

"I need time to think, please leave me alone! Get out!"

Tears streamed down her face as she walked to the door. "Okay, Ray-Ray. If that's what you want, baby.

"I'm sorry, Grandma. I didn't mean to yell at you. I just want to be alone right now. Please try to understand. I love you. I will call you later."

I hugged and kissed her before she left, and I looked in the mirror and saw the bruises on my face where Elliot slapped me. I cried, "What do I do? Lord, please help me. Tell me what I should do?"

My phone rang. I answered immediately without looking. "Hello, Elliot?"

"Nah, it's David, Rayna. Look, you need to get to your grandmother's house immediately! I will explain when I get there in about 3 or 4 hours. Stay away from Elliot! He's gone mad and may seriously hurt you or even kill you!"

"Mr. David, please stop with the nonsense. I know him and understand him. Y'all butt out!"

I hung up the phone and began to pray.

"God give me a sign. Should I leave or stay? He's my husband and I love him. I don't think you mean for a wife to be treated the way he does me. He's so abusive, Lord. I can't take it anymore. I'm so afraid of him.

God help me make the right decision."

CHAPTER 55

INTERVENE, LORD

Grandma Flo cried all the way home. When she went inside, she went into her bedroom, closed the door, and fell to her knees by her bed. She began to pray.

"Oh Lord, my God. I need you to hear me, Father . My granddaughter is blinded by love. The Devil has clouded her judgment. She can't even pray, Lord. I need you to intervene and deliver her from that evil Elliot. Please, Lord, awaken Rayna from her deep sleep. Remind her who you are. Restore her faith, joy, and peace. In Jesus' name. Amen."

There was a knock at the door. When she looked out the window, she ran to the door and flung it open. "Carol, I'm so glad you're here! Hey, James."

"Hey, ladybug! What's wrong?"

"Yeah, Mama. Mr. David said for us to get down here immediately! Something about Ray-Ray being in danger! Where is she?"

"She's not here. She wants to be left alone. She thinks she can handle Elliot. She said she *understands him.*"

Grandma Flo began to cry again. Carol and James comforted her while another knock came at the door. It was Benjamin and Sierra.

"Hi, guys. What's going on?" Sierra asked.

Carol explained, "Well, it looks like Rayna's life is in danger! Mr. David believes Elliot is going to either seriously hurt her or maybe kill her."

"I knew that fool was crazy!" Sierra yelled.

"Calm down, babe." Benjamin hugged her. He looked at Carol and Grandma Flo. "How can we help?"

"We're trying to get her to come over here, but she won't listen. She really thinks she can "fix" Elliot. I told her he had already killed three people." Grandma Flo got up to get a box of Kleenex.

Sierra collapsed into Benjamin's arms, crying, "We have to get her. I have to save her!"

James held Carol and said, "We have to pray about this. The Lord doesn't want us to take matters into our own hands. Let's just let the police handle it."

"No disrespect, Dad, but sometimes the Lord sends help and answers prayer quickly. I think I may be that "help" to get Elliot before the police do."

"Son, don't do that. 'Vengeance is mine saith the Lord.' Be patient. They'll get him."

"We can't sit around here and do nothing!" shouted Sierra. "I'm going over there!"

"No, you're not, babe. Not without me." Benjamin butted in.

"Well, come on then!"

They stood up to leave when a knock was at the door. Mr. David was nearly out of breath. They ran past him without a word.

Chapter 56

THE CANARY SINGS

Agent Johnson told an officer to bring Drake a sandwich and some coffee. He let Drake know that the confession was being videotaped and recorded. So Agent Johnson and his assistant began the questioning. "Drake Hudson, would you like an attorney present before you make your confession?"

"C'mon man, I just want to get this over with. No, I don't want no lawyer."

"Okay, how'd you meet or come to know Elliot Nolan?"

"Back in high school Elliot's brother, Elijah, and I were friends. Not best friends, you know. Just hung out sometimes. We were both on the football team. I used to let him and Elliot crash at my place a few times. They used to have it out with their Uncle; especially Elliot."

"What do you mean 'especially Elliot?'"

"I think Elliot used to get beat a lot by his Uncle. They were planning on leaving one night and Elijah and his cousin started fighting. Elijah got hit by his Uncle and died. Elliot told me his brother was *'murdered'* by his Uncle James. He said his Uncle got off because he was a pastor or something like that. Elliot couldn't let it go though. He said them liars would have a part in his lake. Whatever that is."

"How'd you get involved with Elliot's schemes, Drake? I mean, you seem like a smart young man."

"I *am* a smart young man. I messed up in college with football and needed some dough. Elliot said he needed some cameras installed at some girl's house that he had been checking out for a while. I told him I would do it if the price was right. He gave me $25,000 the first time."

"The first time?"

"Yeah. For the other jobs, I upped the price. I mean, it's not like he didn't have the money. His parents left him and Elijah well off. He even got Elijah's share of the money since Elijah was dead."

"Did Elliot kill his aunt and cousins?"

"Hey man, I wasn't there. I don't know for sure about the aunt. I mean, he did talk to me about the cousins, but I told him I ain't going out like that. I said the most the cops could get me for was installing them cameras illegally."

"Uh wrong, my friend. You're also under arrest for obstruction of justice and for impeding an investigation."

CHAPTER 57

GET ME OUT!

I received a call from Elliot and he sounded ticked off. "So you made it back, huh? We ain't finished talking, Rayna." He hung up.

I looked at my face in the mirror again. My eyes were swollen from crying so much. The bruises were more evident now. I thought to myself, "How long am I going to keep waiting for him to change? God gives everyone chances and choices. Do I want to settle for *a piece of a man* just to say "At least I have a man" or do I want to live a peaceful life as a single woman?

At that moment, I realized, that God answered my prayer! I **need to**...No! I **have to** get out of this toxic relationship because it's not worth my life; my happiness, my peace. I can barely focus on Christ or myself and well being.

I started packing at once when I heard footsteps. The key turned, and I ran into the kitchen.

Elliot slammed the door. He saw that my bags were packed and the wedding ring was on the kitchen island.

"Seriously? You think you leaving me?!" Elliot yells.

His eyes are full of anger...piercing my very soul. His face is tight. He begins pacing in a circle.

"Did you forget 'til death do us part'? You know I'm not letting you go, right? I'm ready to go join my family, Rayna, and you going with me. You're part of my family. It's time for you to meet my mom, dad, and Elijah."

He walked slowly toward me. Face tight. Fist balled up. He quickly ran to the bedroom and returned with a black, leather belt.

Frantically, I tried to explain that I couldn't take living with him anymore and that everyone was talking about him killing some of his relatives.

But it was like he could no longer hear or see me; as if he was in some hypnotic state. His eyes looked glazed over with evil.

"Elliot!" He was still walking slowly toward me; zombielike. "Elliot! Did you hear what I said?"

Fist closed. He raises the belt. It was wrapped tightly around his fist like brass knuckles. My body was trembling now. I was frozen stiff. My legs wouldn't budge. I couldn't scream! "Run!" I heard my mind telling me, but fear gripped me. I couldn't move. I felt as though I was weighed down by heavy sandbags. I haven't seen him this angry before. And then...

BOP! Right in the mouth! I could almost taste the metal from the belt buckle.

I fell to the floor as if I were in a boxing ring and down for the count. I couldn't get up. It's a knockout! The weight of my body felt heavy. Those massive, muscular hands tightened around my throat, and, he shook me like a rag doll! I was too physically weak to escape his grasp! Warm blood seeped through my teeth. My nose and mouth spurted blood and flooded my throat. I tried not to swallow. I felt faint. Wait! Is that my tooth over there? I must be imagining this! A missing tooth!

I was about to pass out when...

Boom! Boom! Boom! Who's knocking at the door? I try to focus. Whisper. Talk. I know it's my girl! My bestie!

Everything looked dim and blurry around me. I still couldn't speak. My mind was screaming, "Lord, please let it be Sierra! Help me!"

Elliot's strong, masculine hands gradually released my throat. As if a hypnotizer jarred him out of his trance.

Now he was calming down; his monstrous, demonic face looked serene. I could suddenly breathe again! Praise Jesus (as Grandma Flo would say)! I started to cough! My throat and my neck hurt so badly. My feet were extremely sore from trying to fight him off. Every single muscle ached in my small-framed, size 6 body. I wanted to scream but nothing came out. My vocal cords felt strange...swollen; constricted.

Oh no! I think I wet myself!

There was a knock at the door again. This time it's louder. "Dang it!" he says. Seeming frustrated at the interruption. I heard him yell, Who is it?!"

"Hey is Ray-Ray here? I called her several times and she's not answering her phone.

"You betta go on now Sierra! We busy! She'll call you later." Elliot threatened.

Thank God! It's Sierra!

"Fool, open this door! I wanna hear it from her."

With reluctance, Elliot's bloody knuckles unlocked the deadbolt.

He realized the belt was still wrapped around his hand and tossed it across the room. He opened the door with the chain lock still in its place.

I start coughing again. This time I spat out the blood that was lodged in my throat. Something else spurted out along with it. Another tooth?

"Lord, if You get me out of this, I won't go back," I thought to myself.

Oh no! The baby! I begin to rub my stomach and cry. I found out before leaving for the Bahamas and was going to surprise Elliot.

"God, help me, Elliot if you don't open this door! The cops are already on the way! Benjamin called them!"

Elliot slammed the door and jammed it with a chair.

He ran into the bedroom, grabbed a duffle bag, and headed for the window.

He glared back at me wild-eyed and said, "This ain't over, ho! I'm going to get you...just wait!" I passed out as he ran down the fire escape...sirens blaring!

As I lay on the cold, hard marble floor behind the kitchen island, I thought, "Mama, you were wrong about having a 'piece of a man'; I'd rather have peace of mind!"

ABOUT THE AUTHOR

Ruth Hampton was reared in a small, rural town somewhere in NC, USA. As a youngster, she enjoyed writing poetry and later, research essays in college while pursuing her Master of Arts in Teaching Special Education Degree from UNC-Charlotte. Go Niner Nation!

She continues to reside in North Carolina while working as an educator in special education and fulfilling her dream as a self-published author.

Ruth's sources of inspiration and testimony for writing are brought on by her personal experiences from domestic violence and toxic relationships.

One day Ruth prayed to God for deliverance from hating the past detrimental situations that she found herself in and erroneous decisions she made to have and/or keep a man (twice). Yes; even as a Christian, she fell into depression and anxiety. Later, wound up in therapy anon medication—the best decision ever made—without shame or guilt. Ruth believes your mind deserves a tune up just like your car. If ignored over a period of time, it will break down from all the wear and tear.

Remember, the scripture declares, "But when Jesus heard that, he said unto them, They that be whole need not a physician, but they that are sick (Matthew 9:12)." She is a firm believer that God + therapy + medication(if necessary)

= healing. God continued to bring healing when HE told her: "A person has a right to love who and what they want. They just didn't choose you." You might be surprised what you—the wife or significant other—can be left in the dust for besides a mistress. Whether it's power, control, lover of money, alcohol, and/or drugs.

Just like God gives us a chance and a choice to serve him of our own free will, so it is with humans and marriage. It's okay to forgive and let that person go without staying bitter or holding grudges. You do not have to prove anything to anyone when you forgive. God knows and that is all that matters. Keep moving forward now with a peace of mind; embarking on your own journey with God. Your journey is not going to mimic another's; so no explanation is needed as to what yours (journey) may seem like to others.

Though life tosses numerous curveballs, unexpected hills, and deep-trodden valleys towards her, God blesses Ruth to overcome and continue striving to accomplish her passions—writing and authorship. God has instilled an immeasurable portion of faith within Ruth that is "like a tree planted by the rivers of water, that bringeth forth his fruit in his season; his leaf also shall not wither and whatsoever he doeth shall prosper (Psalm 1:3 KJV)."